A Young Doctor's

Notebook

Other books by MIKHAIL BULGAKOV
published by Alma Classics

Black Snow

Diaboliad and Other Stories

Diaries and Selected Letters

A Dog's Heart

The Fatal Eggs

The Life of Monsieur de Molière

The Master and Margarita

Notes on a Cuff and Other Stories

The White Guard

A Young Doctor's Notebook

Mikhail Bulgakov

Translated by Hugh Aplin

ALMA CLASSICS

ALMA CLASSICS
an imprint of

ALMA BOOKS LTD
3 Castle Yard
Richmond TW10 6TF
United Kingdom
www.almaclassics.com

The stories in *A Young Doctor's Notebook* first published in Russian
in 1925–26.
Morphine first published in Russian in 1927.
This translation first published by Alma Classics Ltd (previously
Oneworld Classics Ltd) in 2011
This new edition first published by Alma Classics Ltd in 2012
© by the Estate of Mikhail Bulgakov

Reprinted 2013, 2015, 2017, 2019, 2021

Translation and notes © Hugh Aplin, 2011
Cover © nathanburtondesign.com

Background material © Alma Classics Ltd

Printed in Great Britain by CPI Group (UK) Ltd, Croydon CR0 4YY

ISBN: 978-1-84749-286-9

Contents

Mikhail Bulgakov (1891–1940)

Afanasy Ivanovich Bulgakov,
Bulgakov's father

Varvara Mikhailovna Bulgakova,
Bulgakov's mother

Lyubov Belozerskaya,
Bulgakov's second wife

Yelena Shilovskaya,
Bulgakov's third wife

Москва.—Moscou. № 322.
Садовая Тріумфальная д. Пигитъ.—Sadovaya Maison

Bulgakov's residences on Bolshaya Sadovaya St. (above) and Nashchokinsky Pereulok (bottom left); an unfinished letter to Stalin (bottom right)

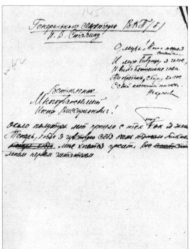

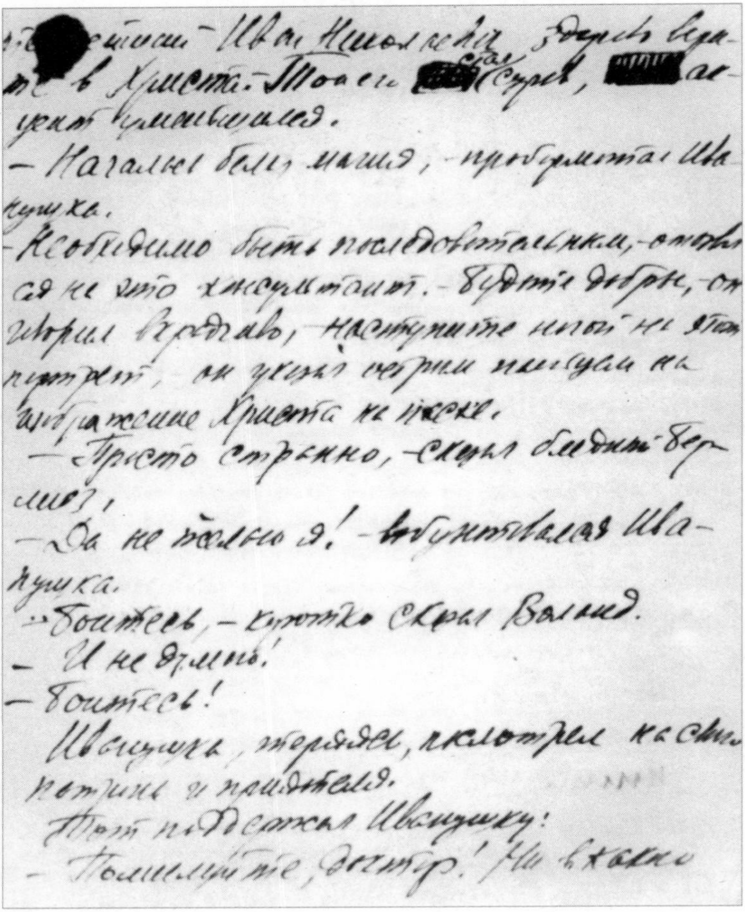
[illegible] — Иван Николаевич, будучи верующим в Христа. — Тоже [redacted] (Берлиоз), [redacted] [illegible].

— Начались бесы, магия, — пробормотал Иванушка.

— Необходимо быть последовательным, — отозвался на это консультант. — Будьте добры, — он говорил вкрадчиво, — наступите ногой на этот портрет, — он указал острым пальцем на изображение Христа на песке.

— Просто странно, — сказал бледный Берлиоз.

— Да не буду я! — взбунтовался Иванушка.

— Боитесь, — коротко сказал Воланд.

— И не думаю!

— Боитесь!

Иванушка, теряясь, посмотрел на своего патрона и приятеля.

Тот поддержал Иванушку:

— Помилуйте, доктор! Ни в каком

An autograph page from *The Master and Margarita*

A Young Doctor's
Notebook

The Towel with
a Cockerel Motif

I F A MAN HAS NEVER travelled in horse-drawn vehicles on remote country roads, there's no point my telling him about it: he won't understand anyway. And for anyone who has, I don't even want to call it to mind.

I'll state briefly: it took me and my driver exactly twenty-four hours to travel the forty versts* that separate the small provincial town of Grachovka from the Muryino Hospital.* And the exactness was even something curious: at two o'clock in the afternoon of 16th September 1917 we were by the last grain-merchant's warehouse on the boundary of that remarkable town of Grachovka, and at five past two on the 17th September of that same unforgettable year of 1917 I was standing on the trampled, dying grass, grown soft in the light September rain, of the Muryino Hospital yard. I stood there looking like this: my legs were ossified, and to such a degree that right there in the yard I was mentally leafing through the pages of textbooks, obtusely trying to remember whether there really did exist, or whether I had imagined it in my sleep in the village of Grabilovka the night before, an illness in which a man's muscles become ossified. What was the damned thing called in Latin? Each of those muscles ached with an unbearable pain reminiscent of toothache. I hardly need mention my toes – inside my boots they no longer moved, they lay quiet, they were like wooden stumps. I confess that in a surge of faint-heartedness I whispered a curse on medicine and the application I had submitted to the rector of the university five years before. Rain was sprinkling down from on high at that moment as if through a sieve. My overcoat had swollen up like a sponge. In vain did I attempt to grab hold of the handle of my suitcase with the fingers of my right hand, and finally I spat on the wet grass. My fingers were unable to catch hold of anything, and being stuffed with all sorts of knowledge from interesting medical books, I again recalled an illness – palsy.

"Paralysis," I said to myself mentally, despairingly, and the devil knows why.

"One has to g-get used," I began with wooden, blue lips, "to t-travelling on your roads."

And at the same time I for some reason stared angrily at the driver, although he personally wasn't in the least to blame for the road.

"Blimey... Comrade Doctor," the driver responded, he too barely moving his lips beneath his little fair moustache, "I've been travelling on 'em for fifteen years, and I still can't get used to 'em."

I shuddered and looked round miserably at the white, two-storeyed hospital building with its peeling paint, at the unwhitewashed log walls of the *feldsher*'s* little house, at my own future residence – a two-storeyed, very clean building with mysterious, funereal windows – and heaved a long sigh. And at once there flashed dimly through my mind not Latin words, but a sweet phrase which, in a brain gone crazy with the rocking and the cold, was sung by a plump tenor with blue thighs:

*...Greetings to you... my sa-cred re-fuge...**

Farewell, farewell for many a long day, to the gold and red Bolshoi Theatre, Moscow, shop windows... ah, farewell.

4

"I'll put on a sheepskin coat next time," I thought in angry despair, trying with unbending hands to wrench the suitcase out by its straps, "I'll... although next time it'll already be October... it'll make no difference if you put on two sheepskin coats. And the soonest I'll be going to Grachovka will be in a month, it will... Just think of it... We actually had to stop for the night! We did twenty versts and found ourselves in sepulchral darkness... night... we had to stop for the night in Grabilovka... the teacher let us in... And we left this morning at seven a.m.... And there you are driving... good heavens... slower than a pedestrian. One wheel crashes into a pothole, the other lifts up in the air, the suitcase plonks down onto your feet... then it's over onto one side, then the other, then it's nose first, then nape first. And down and down comes the rain from on high, and your bones grow cold. Could I possibly have believed that in the middle of a grey, sour September a man can freeze in the fields as if in a harsh winter?! But it does indeed turn out that he can. And while you're dying your slow death, all you see is one and the same thing, just the one. To the right, a field picked bare and with a hump in it, to the left, a stunted coppice, and beside it some grey, ramshackle huts, five or six of them. And there doesn't seem to be a single living soul inside them. Silence, silence all around..."

The suitcase finally yielded. The driver had leant his stomach on it and shoved it out straight at me. I tried to keep hold of it by the strap, but my hand refused to work, and my distended, exasperated travelling companion, with its books and various bits and pieces, flopped straight down onto the grass, giving me a whack on the legs.

"Oh dear Lor..." the driver began in fright, but I made no complaint – my legs were good for nothing anyway.

"Hey, is anybody there? Hey!" the driver shouted, and started clapping his hands, making a noise like a cockerel does with its wings. "Hey, I've brought the doctor!"

At this point faces appeared at the dark window panes of the *feldsher*'s house and pressed up against them; a door slammed, and then I saw a man in an awful torn coat and tatty boots come stumping across the grass towards me. Politely and hurriedly he took off his cap, ran two paces towards me, for some reason gave a bashful smile, and greeted me in a hoarse voice.

"Hello, Comrade Doctor."

"Who are you?" I asked.

"I'm Yegorych," the man introduced himself, "the watchman hereabouts. We've been waiting and waiting for you…"

And at once he grabbed hold of the suitcase, hoisted it up onto his shoulder and carried it off. I began limping after him, trying unsuccessfully to put my hand into my trouser pocket and take out my purse.

In essence, a man needs very little. And what he needs first and foremost is fire. About to head for the backwoods of Muryino, I seem to remember promising myself while still in Moscow that I was going to conduct myself with dignity. To begin with, my youthful appearance poisoned my existence. I had to introduce myself to everyone:

"Dr So-and-so."

And everyone was sure to raise their eyebrows and ask:

"Are you really? And there was I thinking you were still a student."

"No, I've graduated," I would answer sullenly, and think: "I need to get a pair of glasses, that's what." But there was no reason to get a pair of glasses, my eyes were healthy, and their clarity was still unclouded by worldly experience. As I didn't have the option of protecting myself from the customary condescending and tender smiles with the aid of glasses, I tried to develop a particular manner to inspire respect. I attempted to speak in a weighty and measured way, to keep in check as far as possible any impetuous movements,

not to run, the way people do at twenty-three when they're
university graduates, but to walk. As I now understand, after
many years have passed, none of this worked very well at all.

At the moment in question I had violated this, my un-
written code of conduct. I sat hunched up, sat shoeless
in my socks, and sat not somewhere like my study, but in
the kitchen, and, like a fire-worshipper, inspired and passionate, reached out towards the birch logs glowing in the
cooking stove. At my left hand stood an upturned tub, and
on it lay my boots, and next to them lay a plucked, bare-
skinned cockerel with a bloody neck, and in a heap next
to the cockerel lay its multicoloured feathers. The fact is
that, while still stiff with cold, I had managed to perform a
whole series of actions demanded for life itself. Sharp-nosed
Aksinya, Yegorych's wife, I had confirmed in the position
of my cook. And it was in consequence of this that the
cockerel had perished at her hands. I was to eat it. I had
met everyone. The *feldsher* was called Demyan Lukich, the
midwives – Pelageya Ivanovna and Anna Nikolayevna. I had
managed to go round the hospital and had satisfied myself
with the utmost clarity that the stock of instruments it had
was extremely rich. At the same time I was compelled to
admit with the same clarity (to myself, of course) that the
purpose of very many of the virginally shining instruments
was completely unknown to me. Not only had I never held
them in my hands, I had never, I admit it frankly, even seen
them.

"Hm," I mumbled most meaningfully, "you have a marvellous stock of instruments though. Hm…"

"Yes indeed, sir," Demyan Lukich remarked sweetly, "it's
all through the efforts of your predecessor, Leopold Leopoldovich. He was operating from dawn till dusk, you know."

At that point I broke out in a cold sweat and looked miserably at the gleaming plate-glass cabinets.

Thereafter we went round the empty wards, and I satisfied myself that they could accommodate forty people with ease.

"Leopold Leopoldovich sometimes even had fifty in," Demyan Lukich comforted me, while Anna Nikolayevna, a woman wearing a crown of grey hair, said, apropos of something or other:

"You look so young, Doctor, so young. It's simply amazing. You look like a student."

"What the devil," I thought. "Honestly, it's like a conspiracy!"

I muttered through my teeth, drily:

"Hm... no, I... that is, I... yes, I do look young..."

Next we went downstairs to the dispensary, and I immediately saw that it contained everything you could possibly think of. In two darkish rooms there was a strong smell of herbs, and on the shelves stood everything you might want. There were even some foreign patent medicines, and scarcely does it need to be added that I had never heard anything about them.

"Leopold Leopoldovich ordered them," reported Pelageya Ivanovna with pride.

"This Leopold was simply a genius," I thought, and was filled with respect for the mysterious Leopold who had abandoned quiet Murye.

Besides fire, a man also needs to find his feet. I had long since eaten the cockerel, Yegorych had stuffed a hay mattress for me and covered it with a sheet, a lamp was burning in the study in my residence. I sat and, as if spellbound, gazed at the third achievement of the legendary Leopold: the cabinet was stuffed full of books. I cursorily counted about thirty volumes of surgery manuals alone, in Russian and German. And the books on therapy! The wonderful dermatological atlases!

The evening was drawing in, and I was finding my feet.

"I'm not to blame for anything," I thought, stubbornly and agonizingly, "I've got a degree, I have top marks in fifteen exams. And I warned them in advance, while still in that big city, that I wanted to go somewhere as an assistant doctor. No. They smiled and said: 'You'll find your feet.' So much for you'll find your feet. And what if they bring me a hernia? Explain to me how I'll find my feet with that. And in particular, how will the patient with the hernia feel in my hands? He'll find his feet in the next world..." (at this point a chill ran down my spine) "Or what about acute purulent appendicitis? Ha! Or village children with diphtheritic croup? When a tracheotomy's required? And even without a tracheotomy I won't be having it so good... Or... or... childbirth! I'd forgotten about childbirth! Incorrect lies. What ever will I do? Eh? What a frivolous man I am! I should have refused this district. I really should have. They would have got themselves some Leopold or other."

In anguish and in the dusk I paced up and down the room. When I drew level with the lamp, in the window, in the boundless darkness of the fields, I caught a glimpse of my pale visage beside the lights of the lamp.

"I'm like the False Dimitry,"* I thought stupidly all of a sudden, and settled down again at the desk.

I tormented myself in solitude for a couple of hours, carrying on until such time as my nerves could simply no longer endure the terrors I had created. At that point I began to calm down and even to create certain plans.

Right then... The numbers coming to surgery, they say, are insignificant just now. They're breaking flax in the villages, the roads are impassable... "And it's now that they'll bring you a hernia," thundered a stern voice in my brain, "because a man with a cold (an uncomplicated illness) won't travel on impassable roads, but they *will* struggle in here with a hernia, you rest assured, dear colleague Doctor."

The voice wasn't stupid, was it? I winced.

"Be quiet," I said to the voice, "there doesn't *have* to be a hernia. What's this neurasthenia? If a job's once begun, never leave it till it's done."

"You've made your bed, now lie in it," the voice responded snidely.

Right then... I'll never part with my handbook... If something needs to be prescribed, you can think it over while you're washing your hands. The handbook will lie open directly on top of the patient register. I'll write helpful, but uncomplicated prescriptions. Well, for example, one 0.5 sachet of *natrii salicylici* powder three times a day.

"You can prescribe soda!" responded my internal interlocutor, manifestly mocking me.

What's soda got to do with it? I'll prescribe *Cephaelis ipecacuanha* as well – *infusum...*[*] 180. Or two hundred. If you please.

And straight away, although no one was demanding any *ipecacuanha* of me in my solitude by the lamp, I leafed faint-heartedly through the prescription handbook, checked on *ipecacuanha*, and in passing read mechanically about the existence of some stuff "insipin" too. It's none other than "ethereal sulphate of quinine-diglycolic acid"... Apparently it doesn't taste of quinine! But what's it for? And how is it prescribed? What is it – a powder? The devil take it!

"Insipin's all very well, but what will happen with the hernia all the same?" terror in the form of the voice persisted in badgering me.

"I'll sit it down in a bath," I defended myself frenziedly, "in a bath. And I'll try and put it back in place."

"A strangulated one, my angel! What use are baths then, damn it! A strangulated one," sang terror in the voice of a demon. "You have to operate..."

At that point I gave in and almost burst into tears. And I sent an entreaty to the darkness beyond the window: anything you like, only not a strangulated hernia.

And tiredness crooned:

"Go to bed, you ill-starred Aesculapius.* Have a good sleep, and in the morning you'll see. Calm down, you young neurasthenic. Look – the darkness beyond the windows is at peace, the cooling fields are asleep, there is no hernia. And in the morning you'll see. You'll find your feet... Sleep... Put the atlas down... You won't understand a darned thing now anyway. The hernia ring..."

How he had flown in I couldn't even comprehend. I seem to recall that the bolt on the door had made a clatter, and Aksinya had said something in a squeak. And a cart had creaked by outside the windows too.

He was hatless, in an unbuttoned sheepskin jacket, with a tangled little beard and crazed eyes.

He crossed himself and fell to his knees and banged his forehead against the floor. This was to me.

"I'm done for," I thought in anguish.

"What are you doing, what are you doing?" I mumbled, and pulled at his grey sleeve.

His face was contorted, and in reply, choking, he started to mumble some jerky words:

"Mr Doctor... Mr... my only, my only... my only one!" he cried out suddenly in a youthfully resonant voice that made the lampshade quiver. "Oh Lord... Oh..." He wrung his hands in anguish, and again began banging his forehead against the floorboards as though he wanted to crack it open. "Why? Why this punishment?... How have we angered You?"

"What? What's happened?" I cried out, sensing that my face was growing cold.

He leapt to his feet, lurched back and forth, and then this is what he whispered:

"Mr Doctor… whatever you want… I'll give you money… Take the money, as much as you want. As much as you want. We'll bring you food… Only she mustn't die. She mustn't die. If she remains a cripple – so be it. So be it!" he shouted at the ceiling. "There's enough to keep her fed, there's enough."

Aksinya's pale face hung in the black square of the door. Anguish was entwining itself around my heart.

"What?… What? Tell me!" I cried out painfully.

He fell quiet, and in a whisper, as though confidentially, he said to me – and his eyes became fathomless:

"She fell into the brake…"

"The brake, the brake?…" I repeated. "What's that?"

"Flax, they were breaking flax… Mr Doctor…" Aksinya explained in a whisper, "the brake… they're breaking flax…"

"This is the start. This is it. Oh, why did I come?!" I thought in horror.

"Who?"

"My daughter," he replied in a whisper, and then shouted: "Help!" And he fell to the ground once more, and his hair, cut in a fringe, flopped down over his eyes.

The two horns of the kerosene lamp with its crooked tin shade were burning hotly. On the operating table, on a white, fresh-smelling oilcloth, I saw her, and the hernia faded from my memory.

Fair, slightly reddish hair hung down from the table in disorder, dry and matted with *plica polonica*.* The plait was gigantic, and its end was touching the floor.

The cotton skirt was torn to pieces, and the blood on it was of different colours – a brown patch, a rich, scarlet patch. The light of the kerosene lamp seemed to me yellow and alive, and her face like paper, white, with the nose sharpened.

On her white face, motionless, plaster-like, a truly rare beauty was dying away. It's not every day, not often that you'll encounter such a face.

For about ten seconds there was complete silence in the operating room, but outside the closed doors someone could be heard letting out indistinct cries and banging, continually banging their head.

"He's lost his senses," I thought, "so the nurses are giving him a drink... Why such a beauty? Though he does have regular features... The mother was evidently beautiful... He's a widower..."

"Is he a widower?" I whispered mechanically.

"He is," Pelageya Ivanovna replied quietly.

At that point, with an abrupt, almost angry movement, Demyan Lukich tore the skirt apart from bottom to top and all at once laid her bare. I looked, and what I saw exceeded my expectations. The left leg, as such, wasn't there. Starting from the shattered knee, there lay bloody shreds and red, mangled muscles, and poking out sharply in all directions were white, crushed bones. The right one was fractured at the shin in such a way that the ends of both pieces of bone had broken through the skin and come out. Because of this her foot lay lifeless, seemingly apart, turned to one side.

"Yes," said the *feldsher* quietly, and added nothing more.

At that point I emerged from my benumbed state and felt for her pulse. It wasn't there in her cold arm. Only after several seconds did I find a scarcely perceptible, isolated ripple. It passed... then there was a pause, during which I had time to glance at the wings of her nose, which were turning blue, and her white lips... Already I wanted to say: "It's the end..." Fortunately, I restrained myself... The thread-like ripple came again.

"This is how a person torn to pieces dies away," I thought, "there's absolutely nothing you can do here..."

But suddenly, not recognizing my own voice, I said sternly: "Camphor."

At this point Anna Nikolayevna leant towards my ear and whispered:

"Why, Doctor? Don't torment her. Why another injection? She's going to pass away at any moment... You won't save her."

I looked round at her, angry and sullen, and said:

"I'm asking for camphor..."

Such that Anna Nikolayevna, with a flushed, offended face, immediately rushed to the table and broke open an ampoule.

The *feldsher* evidently disapproved of the camphor too. Nonetheless, he deftly and quickly took hold of a syringe and the yellow oil passed under the skin on the shoulder.

"Die. Hurry up and die," I thought, "die. Or else what ever am I going to do with you?"

"She'll be dead in a moment," whispered the *feldsher*, as though he had guessed my thoughts. He threw a sidelong glance at a sheet, but evidently changed his mind: it was a shame to get blood on the sheet. However, a few seconds later she had to be covered up. She was lying like a corpse, but she wasn't dead. Suddenly things in my head became light, like under the glass roof of our distant anatomical theatre.

"More camphor," I said hoarsely.

And again the *feldsher* obediently injected the oil.

"Is she really not going to die?" I thought despairingly. "Am I really going to have to..."

Everything in my brain was lightening, and suddenly, without any textbooks, without advice, without assistance, I understood – with an iron certainty that I *had* understood – that now, for the first time in my life, I was going to have to perform an amputation on a person who was unconscious. And that person was going to die under the knife. She had no blood, after all! In the course of ten versts, everything

14

had flowed out through the shattered legs, and it was even uncertain whether she could feel anything now, whether she could hear. She was silent. Oh, why didn't she die? What would her crazed father say to me?

"Prepare for amputation," I said to the *feldsher* in a voice not my own.

The midwife gave me a wild look, but there was a brief spark of sympathy in the *feldsher*'s eyes, and he started bustling about by the instruments. The Primus let out a roar beneath his hands...

A quarter of an hour passed. With superstitious horror I kept peering into an unconscious eye, lifting the cold lid. I couldn't grasp a thing... How could a semi-corpse be alive? Beads of sweat ran unrestrainedly down my forehead from under my white cap, and Pelageya Ivanovna wiped the salty sweat away with a piece of gauze. Swimming in the remnants of the blood in the girl's veins there was now caffeine too. Should it have been injected or not? Anna Nikolayevna, barely touching, was stroking out the bumps that had swollen up on the hips because of the saline. But the girl was alive.

I picked up a knife, trying to imitate somebody (I had seen an amputation once in my life at university)... I was now begging Fate not to let her die in the next half-hour... "Let her die in the ward when I've finished the operation..."

Only my common sense was working on my behalf, driven on by the extraordinariness of the situation. With an extremely sharp knife, like an experienced butcher, I made a deft, circular slash around the hip, and the skin parted without producing a single droplet of blood. "What will I do if the vessels start bleeding?" I thought, and cast sidelong looks, like a wolf, at a heap of torsion forceps. I cut off an enormous morsel of female meat with one of the blood vessels – it was in the form of a little whitish tube – but not a drop of blood came out of it. I clamped it with torsion forceps and moved on. I clipped the torsion forceps on everywhere that I assumed there to be blood vessels... "*Arteria... arteria...* What the devil's the name?..." The operating room began to look like a clinic. Torsion forceps hung in bunches. They were pulled up and out of the way, along with the meat, with gauze, and with a dazzling, finely serrated saw I began sawing the round bone.

"Why doesn't she die?... It's amazing... oh, how a person clings to life!"

And the bone fell away. Left in Demyan Lukich's hands was what used to be a girl's leg. Tatters, meat, bones! All this was thrown aside, and on the table was a girl, seemingly a third shorter, with a stump pulled away to one side. "Just a little more... don't die," I thought, inspired, "hang on until the ward, let me get out safe and sound from this terrible event in my life."

Then the ligatures were tied, then, clicking the Collin,* I started sewing up the skin with well-spaced stitches... but I stopped as it dawned on me and I realized... I left an outflow... inserted a gauze tampon... Sweat was flooding my eyes, and it seemed to me as though I were in a bathhouse...

I let out a long breath. Looked gravely at the stump, at the waxen face. Asked:

"Alive?"

"Alive..." responded both the *feldsher* and Anna Nikolayevna at once, like a soundless echo.

"She'll live a moment more," the *feldsher* spoke into my ear soundlessly, with his lips alone. Then he hesitated, and tactfully advised: "Perhaps the second leg shouldn't be touched, Doctor. We'll bind it up with gauze... or else she won't make it to the ward... Eh? After all, it's better if she doesn't pass away in the operating room."

"Give me plaster," I responded huskily, prompted by an unknown force.

The entire floor was bespattered with white spots, we were all sweating. The semi-corpse lay motionless. The right leg was bandaged with plaster, and on the shin there yawned the gap I had been inspired to leave at the point of the break.

"She's alive..." croaked the *feldsher* in amazement.

Next we started to lift her, and visible under the sheet was a gigantic void – we left a third of her body in the operating room.

Next there were shadows swaying in the corridor and nurses running up and down, and I saw a dishevelled male figure, which stole along the wall and emitted a dry wail. But he was removed. And it grew quiet.

In the operating room I washed my arms, which were stained with blood up to the elbows.

"You must have performed a lot of amputations, Doctor?" Anna Nikolayevna suddenly asked. "That was very, very good... The equal of Leopold..."

On her lips, the word "Leopold" invariably came out like "doyen".

I glanced from under my brows at their faces. And in all their eyes – in Demyan Lukich's and Pelageya Ivanovna's too – I noted respect and amazement.

"Ahem... I... I've only performed two, actually..."

Why did I lie? I can't understand it now.

It grew quiet in the hospital. Completely.

"When she dies, be sure to send for me," I ordered Demyan Lukich in a low voice, and instead of "very well", he for some reason answered deferentially:

"Yes, sir..."

A few minutes later I was by the green lamp in the study in the doctor's apartment. The house was silent.

A pale face was reflected in the extremely black window pane.

"No, I'm not like Dmitry the Pretender, and, you know, somehow I've aged... There's a line above the bridge of my nose... Somebody will be knocking at any moment... They'll say 'She's dead'..."

Yes, I'll go and take a last look... The knock will come at any moment...

Somebody knocked at the door. It was two and a half months later. One of the first wintry days was shining at the window.

It was he that came in; only now did I look at him closely. Yes, indeed, regular features. About forty-five. Sparkling eyes.

Then a rustling... in on two crutches hopped a one-legged girl of enchanting beauty in an extremely wide skirt, trimmed with a red border around the hem. She looked at me, and her cheeks flushed pink.

"In Moscow... in Moscow..." And I began writing down an address. "They'll arrange a prosthetic there, an artificial leg."

"Kiss his hand," said her father unexpectedly all of a sudden.

I was so flustered that, instead of the lips, I kissed her on the nose.

Then, hanging on her crutches, she undid a package, and out of it fell a long, snow-white towel with an artless red cockerel embroidered on it. So that was what she had been hiding under her pillow during examinations. That's right, I remember, there were cottons on the bedside table.

"I won't take it," I said sternly, and even began shaking my head. But she made such a face, such eyes, that I did take it...

And for many years it hung in my bedroom in Muryino, and then it went with me on my wanderings. Finally it grew ragged, faded, became full of holes, and finally disappeared, fading and disappearing just like memories.

Baptism by Version

T HE DAYS SPED BY in the hospital at N***, and little by little I began to get used to my new life.

In the villages they were breaking flax as before, the roads remained impassable, and I had no more than five people coming to the surgery at a time. My evenings were completely free, and I dedicated them to sorting out the library, to reading textbooks on surgery, and to long, solitary tea-drinking sessions by the softly singing samovar.

It poured with rain for days and nights on end, raindrops tapped incessantly on the roof, and water gushed outside the window, flowing down the guttering into a butt. Out of doors there was slush and mist, a black haze, in which the lights of the windows of the *feldsher*'s house and the kerosene lamp by the gates were just dim, indistinct spots.

On one such evening I was sitting in my study reading an atlas of topographical anatomy. There was complete silence all around, broken only by the occasional gnawing of mice behind the sideboard in the dining room.

I read until my eyelids grew heavy and began to stick together. Finally I yawned, put the atlas aside and decided to go to bed. Stretching, and looking forward to sleeping peacefully to the noise of the rain and its tapping, I went over to the bedroom, undressed and went to bed.

I had not managed to touch the pillow before there swam up in the sleepy gloom in front of me the face of Anna Prokhorova, a seventeen-year-old from the village of To-porovo. Anna Prokhorova needed a tooth pulling. Demyan

19

Lukich, the *feldsher*, floated by noiselessly with a pair of shiny pincers in his hands. I remembered the way he said "suchlike" rather than "such" out of a love for high-flown style, grinned and fell asleep.

However, no more than half an hour later I suddenly woke up, as though somebody had given me a tug. I sat up and, peering fearfully into the darkness, began to listen hard.

Somebody was drumming insistently and loudly on the front door, and I immediately thought the blows ominous.

It was someone knocking at my apartment.

The knocking stopped, there was the clatter of the bolt, I heard the voice of the cook and someone else's unclear voice in reply, then somebody came creaking up the stairs, walked quietly past the study and knocked at the bedroom.

"Who is it?"

"It's me," a deferential whisper answered me, "me, Aksinya, the nurse."

"What's the matter?"

"Anna Nikolayevna's sent for you, says you're to go to the hospital quickly."

"What's happened, then?" I asked, and distinctly felt my heart miss a beat.

"There's a woman been brought from Dultsevo. Her labour's not going well."

"So that's it! It's started!" flashed through my mind, and I was quite unable to get my feet into my slippers. "Oh damn! The matches won't light. Oh well, sooner or later this was bound to happen. You can't just have laryngitis and intestinal catarrh cases all your life."

"Very well. Go and say I'll be there in a moment!" I shouted, and got up from the bed. The shuffling of Aksinya's footsteps began outside the door, and once again there was the clatter of the bolt. Sleep slipped away in an instant. Hurriedly, with trembling fingers, I lit the lamp and began to get dressed. Half-past eleven. What was the matter with this woman whose labour wasn't going well? Hm... an incorrect lie... a narrow pelvis. Or perhaps something worse. Who knows, forceps might have to be used. Should I send her away, straight to town? No, that's unthinkable! A fine doctor, to be sure, everyone will say! And I have no right to do such a thing. No, I have to do it myself. But do what? The devil knows. It'll be awful if I'm at a loss: disgraced in front of the midwives. Still, I need to have a look first, there's no point in worrying before the event.

I got dressed, threw on my overcoat and, hoping in my mind that everything would turn out all right, ran in the rain over slapping planks to the hospital. In the semi-darkness by the entrance a cart was visible, and the horse gave a knock with a hoof on the rotten boards.

"You, was it, that brought the woman in labour?" I for some reason asked the figure stirring beside the horse.

"It was... indeed it was, sir," a peasant woman's voice answered mournfully.

Inside the hospital, despite the late hour, there was animation and bustle. There was a twinkling kerosene lamp burning in the surgery. In the little corridor leading to the delivery room Aksinya rushed past me with a basin. From behind the door there suddenly came a weak groan, which then died away. I opened the door and entered the delivery room. The small, whitewashed room was brightly lit by an overhead lamp. On the bed next to the operating table lay a young woman, covered up to the chin with a blanket. Her face was contorted in a painful grimace, and wet strands of hair were stuck to her forehead. Anna Nikolayevna, with thermometer in hand, was preparing a solution in an Esmarch mug,* while the second midwife, Pelageya Ivanovna, was getting clean sheets out of a cupboard. The *feldsher* stood leaning against the wall in a Napoleonic pose. Upon seeing me, they all stirred themselves. The woman in labour opened her eyes, wrung her hands and started groaning again, mournfully and heavily.

"Well, what's the matter?" I asked, surprising myself with my tone, so confident and calm was it.

"A transverse lie," answered Anna Nikolayevna quickly, continuing to add water to the solution.

"Ri-ight," I drawled, frowning, "well, let's have a look..."

"The doctor needs to wash his hands! Aksinya!" shouted Anna Nikolayevna at once. Her face was solemn and serious.

While the water was flowing and washing the foam from my hands, reddened by the brush, I asked Anna Nikolayevna some insignificant questions, such as how long it was since the woman had arrived and where she was from... Pelageya Ivanovna's hand threw back the blanket, and, sitting on the edge of the bed, with a light touch I started feeling the swollen belly. The woman was groaning, stretching herself out, digging her fingers into the sheet and crumpling it up.

"Gently does it, gently does it... a little longer," I said, laying my hands carefully on the taut, hot, dry skin.

Strictly speaking, after the experienced Anna Nikolayevna had told me what was the matter, this examination was completely unnecessary. However lengthy my examination, I wouldn't in any case learn more than Anna Nikolayevna. Her diagnosis was, of course, correct. A transverse lie. There was the diagnosis. Well, what next?...

Frowning, I continued feeling her belly from all sides and threw sidelong glances at the midwives' faces. Both of them were concentratedly serious, and in their eyes I read approval of my actions. My movements were, indeed, confident and correct, and I was trying to hide my disquiet as deep as possible and not display it in any way.

"Right," I said with a sigh, and I rose from the bed, as there was nothing more to look at from the outside, "let's examine things on the inside."

Again there was a glimpse of approval in Anna Nikolayevna's eyes.

"Aksinya!"

Again the water began to flow.

"Oh dear, if only I could read a bit of Döderlein* now!" I thought miserably, soaping my hands. Alas, to do that now was impossible. And how would Döderlein have helped me at that moment? I washed off the thick foam and painted my fingers with iodine. A clean sheet crackled under Pelageya Ivanovna's hands, and bending towards the woman, I cautiously and timidly began to conduct an internal examination. A picture involuntarily surfaced in my memory of the operating theatre in the obstetrical clinic. Brightly burning electric lamps in opaque globes, a shiny tiled floor, sparkling taps and apparatus everywhere. A junior teacher in a snow-white coat is manipulating a woman in labour, and there are three house surgeons around him to assist, probationer doctors, a crowd of students. Nice, light and safe.

Whereas here am I, all on my own, with a suffering woman on my hands; I am responsible for her. But I don't know how she should be helped, because I have only seen childbirth close up twice in my life in the clinic, and those instances were perfectly normal. Now here I am carrying out an examination, but it's making things no easier either for me or for the woman in labour; I understand precisely nothing, and I can detect precisely nothing there inside her.

And it's already time to decide upon something.

"A transverse lie... as we've got a transverse lie, that means we need to... we need to perform a..."

"Podalic version,"* Anna Nikolayevna was unable to restrain herself, and made the remark as though to herself.

An old, experienced doctor would have looked at her askance for butting in early with her conclusions... But I'm not a man to take offence...

"Yes," I confirmed weightily, "a podalic version."

And pages of Döderlein flashed before my eyes. Internal version... combined version... external version...

Pages, pages... and on them drawings. A basin, contorted, crushed babies with huge heads... an arm hanging down, and on it a noose.

And it was just recently, was it not, that I'd been reading it. And underlining things, thinking carefully about every word, imagining in my mind the correlation of the parts and all the moves. And as I was reading, it had seemed as if the entire text was being imprinted on my brain for ever.

But now, of all that I had read, it was just the one phrase that came to the surface:

A transverse lie is an utterly inauspicious one.

What's true is true. Utterly inauspicious, both for the woman herself, and also for the doctor who had graduated just six months before.

"Well then... let's perform it," I said, rising.

Anna Nikolayevna's face became animated.

"Demyan Lukich," she addressed herself to the *feldsher*, "prepare the chloroform."

It was a very good thing she said this, for otherwise I was still unsure whether or not the operation was performed under anaesthetic! Yes, under anaesthetic, of course – how ever else!

But all the same, I needed to look through Döderlein.

And after washing my hands I said:

"All right, then... you get things ready for the anaesthetic, get her lying down, and I'll be back in a moment, I'll just get my cigarettes from the house."

"Very well, Doctor, there's plenty of time," replied Anna Nikolayevna.

I wiped my hands, the nurse threw my coat onto my shoulders and, without putting my arms into the sleeves, I ran home.

At home in the study I lit the lamp and, forgetting to take my hat off, rushed to the bookcase.

There it is – Döderlein. *Operative Obstetrics*. I hurriedly started rustling the glossy pages.

...version is always a dangerous operation for the mother...

A chill ran down my back, along the spine.

...The main danger is the possibility of spontaneous rupture of the uterus.

Spon-ta-ne-ous...

...If, on introducing his hand into the uterus, the obstetrician has difficulty reaching the foot because of insufficient space or as a result of contraction of the uterine walls, he should refrain from any further attempts at performing the version...

All right. Even if by some miracle I'm able to recognize these "difficulties" and refrain from "further attempts", what, one wonders, am I going to do with the chloroformed woman from the village of Dultsevo?

Carrying on:

...It is absolutely impermissible to attempt to reach the feet along the foetus's back...

We'll bear that in mind.

...Taking hold of the upper leg must be considered errone-ous, since this can easily result in the axial twisting of the foetus, which can give rise to serious battering of the foetus and, as a result, to the most grievous consequences...

"Grievous consequences". Rather vague, but what striking words! And what if the Dultsevo woman's husband is left a widower? I wiped the perspiration on my brow, summoned up my strength and, omitting all the dreadful bits, tried to memorize only the most essential thing: what I actually had to do, how and where I had to introduce my hand. But skimming over the black lines, I came across new dreadful things all the time.

I couldn't help but notice them.

...in view of the enormous danger of rupture... internal and combined version are operations which must be re-garded as among the most dangerous obstetric operations for the mother...

And for a finale:

...With every hour of delay the danger increases...

Enough! The reading had borne fruit: everything had got completely muddled up in my head, and I became convinced in an instant that I understood nothing and, first and fore-most, exactly what sort of version I was going to be doing: a combined one, non-combined, internal, external!...

I gave up on Döderlein and lowered myself into an arm-chair, making an effort to put my scattered thoughts in order... Then I looked at the clock. Damn! It transpired that I'd already been at home for twelve minutes. And over there they were waiting.

...With every hour of delay...

Hours are made up of minutes, and minutes in such instances fly by like crazy. I flung Döderlein down and ran back to the hospital.

There, everything was already prepared. The *feldsher* was standing by the table, on which he was making ready a mask and a phial of chloroform. The woman was already lying on the operating table. Incessant groaning could be heard throughout the hospital.

"Hold on, hold on," muttered Pelageya Ivanovna gently, bending towards the woman, "the doctor will help you in a moment."

"O-oh! Not got... the strength... I've not got the strength!... I can't bear it!"

"Don't worry... Don't worry..." muttered the midwife, "you will bear it! We'll give you something to sniff in a moment... You won't feel a thing."

Water started flowing noisily from the taps, and Anna Nikolayevna and I began cleaning and washing our hands and arms, bared to the elbow. To the accompaniment of the groaning and shrieks, Anna Nikolayevna told me how my predecessor – an experienced surgeon – used to do version. I listened to her avidly, trying not to miss a word. And those ten minutes were more help to me than everything I had read on obstetrics for the state exams, in which I had been awarded a top mark for that very obstetrics. From fragmentary words, unfinished phrases, hints dropped in passing, I learnt those most essential things that are never in any books. And by the time I began wiping my ideally white, clean hands with sterile gauze, resolution had taken hold of me, and in my head there was an absolutely definite, firm plan. Combined or non-combined, I didn't even need to think about that now.

All those technical terms were of no use at that moment. One thing was important: I had to introduce one hand, assist version from the outside with the other, and relying not on books, but on a sense of proportion, without which a doctor is unfit for anything, cautiously but firmly bring one foot down, and by that foot extract the baby.

I had to be calm and cautious, and at the same time boundlessly resolute, unafraid.

"Go ahead," I commanded the *feldsher*, and began rubbing iodine onto my fingers.

Pelageya Ivanovna immediately put the woman's hands together, while the *feldsher* covered her tormented face with the mask. From a dark-yellow phial he began slowly dripping chloroform. A sweet and nauseating smell began to fill the room. The faces of the *feldsher* and the midwives became stern, as though inspired…

"Ga-ah! Ah!" the woman suddenly cried out. She struggled spasmodically for several seconds, trying to throw off the mask.

"Hold her!"

Pelageya Ivanovna grabbed the woman's hands and put them together, pressing them down against her chest. The woman cried out several times more, turning her face away from the mask. But more rarely… more rarely… and in a muffled voice she mumbled:

"Ga-ah… let me go!… Ah!…"

Then ever more weakly, more weakly. Now there was silence in the white room. Transparent drops kept falling, falling onto the white gauze.

"Pelageya Ivanovna, pulse?"

"It's fine."

Pelageya Ivanovna lifted the woman's hand and then released it; lifelessly, like a whip, it slapped down onto the sheets. Moving the mask away, the *feldsher* looked at one of her pupils.

"She's asleep."

A pool of blood. My arms covered in blood up to the elbows. Bloodstains on the sheets. Red clots and balls of gauze. But Pelageya Ivanovna is already shaking the baby and slapping it. Aksinya is making a clatter with buckets, pouring water into basins. The baby is dipped first into cold, then into hot water. It is silent, and its head is swinging lifelessly from side to side as though on a string. But then suddenly, not exactly a squeak, not exactly a sigh, and after it a weak, hoarse, first cry.

"It's alive... it's alive..." Pelageya Ivanovna mutters, and lays the baby down on a pillow.

The mother is alive too. Fortunately, nothing terrible has happened. Now I feel her pulse for myself. Yes, it's regular and distinct, and the *feldsher* gently shakes the woman's shoulder and says:

"Come on, lady, wake up, lady."

The bloodied sheets are thrown aside and the mother is hastily covered with a clean one, and the *feldsher* and Aksinya carry her off to the ward. The swaddled baby rides off on the pillow. The wrinkled little brown face looks out from a white frame, and there is an uninterrupted, thin, piteous squealing.

Water runs from the taps of the washbasins. Anna Nikolayevna draws greedily on a cigarette, screws up her eyes at the smoke, coughs.

"You did the version well, Doctor, with real confidence."

I scrub my hands zealously with a brush and cast sidelong glances at her: is she having a laugh? But on her face is a sincere expression of proud satisfaction. My heart is full of joy. I look at the bloody and white disorder all around, at the red water in the basin, and feel like a victor. But somewhere deep down there stirs a worm of doubt.

"We'll have to see what happens next," I say.

Anna Nikolayevna looks up at me swiftly in surprise.

"What on earth might happen? Everything's all right."

I mumble something indefinite in reply. Strictly speaking, this is what I want to say: is the mother in one piece, did I not do her any harm during the operation... That is what is vaguely tormenting my heart. But my knowledge of obstetrics is so unclear, so bookishly fragmentary! A rupture? And how should that manifest itself? And when will it give notice of itself – straight away, or maybe later?... No, better not open that subject up.

"Well, you never know," I say, "the possibility of infection can't be ruled out," repeating the first phrase to come into my head from some textbook.

"Oh, tha-at," Anna Nikolayevna drawls calmly. "Well, God willing, there'll be nothing of the sort. And where might it come from? Everything's sterile, clean."

It was just after one o'clock when I got home. In a patch of lamplight on the desk in the study Döderlein lay peacefully open at the page 'The Dangers of Version'. I sat with it for another hour or so, gulping tea that had grown cold, leafing through its pages. And now something interesting happened: all of the formerly obscure bits became completely comprehensible, as though they had filled with light, and there, in the light of the lamp, at night, in the back of beyond, I realized what real knowledge means.

"There's great experience to be gained in the countryside," I thought, falling asleep, "only I have to read, read a lot... read..."

The Steel Throat

A ND SO, I WAS LEFT ALONE. Around me were the November darkness and swirling snow, the house was buried, and there was a howling in the chimneys. I'd lived all twenty-four years of my life in an enormous city and had thought that a blizzard howled only in novels. As it turned out, it really did howl. The evenings here were extraordinarily long, the lamp under its blue shade was reflected in the black window, and as I looked at the shiny spot to my left, I dreamt. I dreamt of the local town – it was forty versts away from me. I wanted to go there very much, to escape from my surgery. There was electricity there, four doctors, you could ask their advice, and at least things weren't so frightening. But there was no chance whatsoever of escaping, and I realized myself at times that this was faint-heartedness. After all, this was precisely why I had studied in the medical faculty…

"…Well, and what if a woman's brought in with her labour going wrong? Or, let's suppose, a sick man with a strangulated hernia? What will I do? Be so kind, do give me some advice. Forty-eight days ago I graduated from the faculty with a distinction, but a distinction is one thing, and a hernia is quite another. I saw a professor operating on a strangulated hernia once. He was operating, and I was sitting in the amphitheatre. And that was it…"

Cold sweat repeatedly ran down my spinal column at the thought of a hernia. Every evening, after drinking my fill of tea, I would sit in one and the same pose: by my left hand lay all the manuals on operative obstetrics, with little Döderlein on the top. And to the right there were ten different volumes on operative surgery, with drawings. I would grunt, smoke and drink cold black tea...

And there I was, asleep: I remember the night extremely well – 29th November – and I woke up because of a racket at the door. Some five minutes later, putting on my trousers, I couldn't take my beseeching eyes off those divine books on operative surgery. I could hear the crunch of runners in the yard: my ears had become extraordinarily sharp. What had happened was perhaps even more frightening than a hernia or a baby in a transverse lie: at eleven o'clock at night, a little girl had been brought to me here at the Nikolskoye surgery. The nurse had said in a muffled voice:

"A weak little girl, she's dying... Please come to the hospital, Doctor..."

I remember cutting across the yard, heading for the kerosene lamp by the hospital entrance and watching it twinkling like a man spellbound. The surgery was already lit, and the full complement of my assistants was awaiting me, already dressed and wearing gowns. They were the *feldsher*, Demyan Lukich, still a young man, but very capable, and two experienced midwives, Anna Nikolayevna and Pelageya Ivanovna. And I was a mere twenty-four-year-old doctor who had left university two months before and been appointed to run the Nikolskoye Hospital.

The *feldsher* solemnly threw open the door and the mother appeared. She seemed to fly in, sliding in her felt boots, and the snow on her headscarf hadn't yet melted. In her arms was a package, and it was rhythmically hissing and whistling. The mother's face was contorted, she was crying soundlessly. When she threw off her sheepskin coat and headscarf and unwound the package, I saw a little girl of about three. I looked at her, and for a time I forgot about operative surgery, loneliness, my worthless baggage from university, forgot

32

absolutely everything because of the little girl's beauty. With what could she be compared? Such children are only drawn on chocolate boxes – the hair curls naturally into big rings of almost ripe rye. The most enormous blue eyes, cheeks like a doll's. Angels were drawn like that. But there was a strange opacity nestling in the depths of her eyes, and I realized that this was terror – she couldn't breathe. "She'll be dead in an hour," I thought with utter certainty, and my heart contracted painfully...

With every breath, hollows were being sucked in on her throat, her veins were swelling up and the colour of her face was changing from pinkish to a slightly violet hue. I immediately understood and evaluated this colouring. I grasped what was the matter at once, and I got my diagnosis perfectly right first time, and, most importantly, simultaneously with the midwives – and *they* were experienced. "The girl has diphtheritic croup, her throat's already blocked with layers of membrane, and soon it will close up completely..."

"How many days has the girl been ill?" I asked amidst the guarded silence of my staff.

"Five days, five," said the mother, and looked at me intently with dry eyes.

"Diphtheritic croup," I said through my teeth to the *feldsher*, and to the mother I said: "What on earth were you thinking of? What were you thinking of?"

And at that moment a tearful voice rang out behind me: "Five, sir, five!"

I turned and saw a noiseless, round-faced old woman in a headscarf. "It'd be a good thing if there were none of these old women in the world at all," I thought with a melancholy premonition of danger, and said:

"You shut up, woman, you're being a nuisance." And to the mother I repeated: "What were you thinking of? Five days? Eh?"

Suddenly, with an automatic movement, the mother passed the girl to the old woman and knelt down in front of me.

"Give her some drops," she said, and struck her forehead on the floor, "I'll hang myself if she dies."

"Get up this minute," I replied, "or else I won't even talk to you."

The mother quickly got up with her wide skirt rustling, took the little girl from the old woman and began rocking her. The old woman started praying to the doorpost, and the girl continued to breathe with a snake-like hissing.

The *feldsher* said:

"It's what they all do. The people." And at this his moustache twisted to one side.

"Well, so she's going to die, is she?" asked the mother, gazing at me, or so I thought, in black fury.

"She is," I said, softly and firmly.

The other woman immediately pulled up the hem of her skirt and started wiping her eyes with it. And the mother shouted at me in a dire voice:

"Give them to her, help! Give her some drops!"

I could clearly see what awaited me, and I was firm.

"And what drops am I going to give her? You tell me. The girl's suffocating, her throat's already blocked. You've been killing the little girl for five days, fifteen versts away from me. And what would you have me do now?"

"You're the one should know, sir," the other woman began whining in an unnatural voice at my left shoulder, and immediately I hated her.

"Shut up!" I said to her. And turning to the *feldsher*, I told him to take the girl. The mother handed her to one of the midwives; the girl began struggling, and evidently wanted to shriek, but her voice would no longer come out. The mother tried to shield the girl, but we pushed her aside, and by the light of the kerosene lamp I was able to look into the girl's throat. I had never seen diphtheria until then, apart from minor and quickly forgotten cases. In her throat there was something bubbling, white, ragged. The girl suddenly breathed out and spat in my face, but for some reason, occupied with my thoughts, I wasn't worried about my eyes.

"Now look," I said, amazed at my own calmness, "this is how things stand. It's a late stage. The girl's dying. And nothing can help her, except for one thing – an operation." And I myself was horrified – why had I said that? But I couldn't avoid saying it. "And what if they consent?" the thought occurred to me.

"What do you mean?" asked the mother.

"I'll have to cut her throat open lower down and insert a silver tube to give the girl a chance to breathe, and then perhaps we can save her," I explained.

The mother looked at me as if I were mad, and shielded the girl from me with her arms, and the old woman began jabbering again:

"What are you saying?! Don't let him cut her up! What are you saying? Her throat?!"

"Go away, woman," I said to her with hatred. "Inject the camphor," I said to the *feldsher*.

The mother wouldn't let us have the girl when she saw the syringe, but we explained to her that it was nothing to worry about.

"Perhaps that'll help her?" the mother asked.

"It won't help her in the slightest."

At this point the mother began sobbing.

"Stop it," I said, taking out my watch and adding: "I'll give you five minutes to think. If you don't consent, after five minutes I myself won't undertake to do it."

"I don't consent!" the mother said sharply.

"You don't have our consent!" added the old woman.

35

"Well, as you wish," I added in a muffled voice, and thought: "Well, that's it then! That makes it easier for me. I told them, made the offer, there's astonishment in the midwives' eyes. They've refused and I'm saved."

And no sooner had I thought this than someone else said on my behalf in a voice not my own:

"What, are you mad? What do you mean, you don't consent? You're condemning the girl to die. Consent. Have you no pity?"

"No!" the mother cried once more.

This is what I was thinking inside myself: "What am I doing? I mean, I'm going to kill the girl." But I said something else:

"Come on, hurry, hurry up and consent! Consent! Her fingernails are already turning blue."

"No! No!"

"Well, all right then, take them to the ward, let them sit there."

They were led away through the semi-darkness of the corridor. I could hear the crying of the women and the hissing of the girl.

The *feldsher* returned at once and said:

"They consent!"

All my insides turned to stone, but I pronounced clearly:

"Sterilize a knife, scissors, hooks and a probe at once!"

A minute later I ran across the yard, where the snowstorm was swishing and flying about like a demon, ran to my study and, counting the minutes, grabbed a book, leafed through it and found a drawing illustrating a tracheotomy. Everything in the drawing was clear and straightforward: the throat was opened up and a knife thrust into the windpipe. I started to read the text, but didn't understand a thing, the words seemed to be jumping about before my eyes. I had never seen a tracheotomy done. "Oh, it's too late now," I thought;

I glanced miserably at the blue colour, at the bright draw-ing, and felt that a difficult, terrible job had come crashing down on me; I went back to the hospital without noticing the blizzard.

In the surgery a shadow with round skirts attached itself to me, and a voice started whining:

"How can that be, sir, cutting a little girl's throat? Isn't that unthinkable? *She* consented, the stupid woman. But you don't have my consent, no. I consent to treating her with drops, but I won't let you cut her throat."

"Get this old woman out of here!" I shouted, and added bad-temperedly: "You, you're the stupid woman! You are! And she's actually intelligent! And no one's asking you anyway! Get her out of here!"

One of the midwives put her arms firmly around the old woman and pushed her out of the ward.

"Ready!" said the *feldsher* suddenly.

We went into the small operating room, and, as if through a veil, I saw the shining instruments, the dazzling lamp, the oilcloth... I went out for the last time to the mother, and I was barely able to tear the girl from her arms. I heard only a hoarse voice, which said: "My husband's away. He's in town. When he comes back and finds out what I've done, he'll kill me!"

"He'll kill her," the old woman repeated, gazing at me in horror.

"Don't let them into the operating room!" I ordered.

We remained alone in the operating room. The staff, the girl – Lidka – and I. She sat naked on the table, crying sound-lessly. She was pushed back onto the table and held down, her throat was washed and rubbed with iodine, and I picked up the knife, at the same time thinking: "What am I doing?" The operating room was very quiet. I took the knife and drew a vertical line down her chubby white throat. Not a single drop of blood appeared. I drew the knife a second time down the white strip which had appeared in the parted skin. Again, not one droplet of blood. Slowly, trying to remember some of the drawings in atlases, using a blunt probe I began to separate the fine tissues. And then dark blood came gushing up from somewhere at the base of the wound, instantly flooding it entirely and flowing down the neck. The *feldsher* began wiping it away with tampons, but it didn't abate. Remembering everything I had seen at university, I began squeezing the edges of the wound with forceps, but nothing came of it. I began to feel cold, and my forehead grew damp. I felt acute regret about having entered the medical faculty and about having ended up in these backwoods. In angry despair I thrust the forceps somewhere towards the wound at random, clicked them together, and the blood immediately stopped flowing. We swabbed the wound off with balls of gauze, and it presented itself to me, clean and utterly incomprehensible. There was no windpipe anywhere. My wound didn't resemble any drawing. Two or three more minutes passed, during which I quite mechanically and muddle-headedly dug around in the wound, now with the knife, now with the probe, searching for the windpipe. And by the end of the second minute I had despaired of finding it.

"This is the end," I thought. "Why did I do this? After all, I could have avoided suggesting the operation and had Lidka die quietly in the ward, but now she's going to die with her throat torn apart, and there's no way I can ever prove that she would have died anyway, that I couldn't do her any harm..." One of the midwives silently wiped my forehead. "Put the knife down and say I don't know what to do next," that's what I thought, and I pictured the mother's eyes. I picked the knife up again and senselessly made an abrupt, deep slash in Lidka's throat. The tissues slid apart, and before me unexpectedly was the windpipe.

"Hooks!" I tossed out huskily.

The *feldsher* handed them to me. I thrust one hook in on one side, another on the other, and passed one of them to the *feldsher*. Now I could see only one thing: the greyish ringlets of the pipe. I stuck a sharp knife into the pipe – and froze. The pipe had come up out of the wound, and the *feldsher*, or so it flashed through my mind, had gone mad: he had suddenly started ripping it out. Behind my back both midwives gasped. I raised my eyes and realized what was the matter: it turned out that the *feldsher* had started to fall into a faint because it was so airless, and not having let go of the hook, he was ripping at the windpipe. "Everything's against me, Fate," I thought, "we're sure to have cut Lidka's throat now," and I added to myself sternly: "As soon as I get home, I'll shoot myself..." At this point the senior midwife, evidently very experienced, darted towards the *feldsher* in a predatory sort of way and took the hook away from him, saying as she did so, with her teeth clenched:

"Carry on, Doctor..."

The *feldsher* fell down with a bang as he struck himself, but we didn't look at him. I stuck the knife into the windpipe, then inserted a silver tube. It slipped in neatly, but Lidka remained motionless. The air hadn't gone into her windpipe as required. I heaved a deep sigh and stopped: there was nothing more for me to do. I felt like begging someone's pardon, repenting of my frivolousness, of having entered the medical faculty. There was silence. I could see Lidka turning blue. I already wanted to drop everything and burst into tears, but then suddenly Lidka gave a wild shudder and flung out a fountain of horrible clots of blood through the tube; the air entered her windpipe with a hiss, then the girl started to breathe and began bawling. At that instant the *feldsher* half-rose, pale and sweaty, looked dully at her throat in horror and started to help me sew it up.

In a dream, and through a shroud of sweat that dimmed my eyes, I saw the happy faces of the midwives, and one of them said to me:

"That was brilliant, Doctor, the way you performed the operation."

I thought she was making fun of me, and glanced at her gloomily from under my brows. Then the doors flew wide open, and there was a breath of freshness. Lidka was carried out in a sheet, and at once her mother appeared in the doorway. Her eyes were like the eyes of a wild beast. She asked me:

"Well?"

When I heard the sound of her voice, sweat started running down my back; only then did I grasp how it would have been if Lidka had died on the table. But in a very calm voice I answered her:

"You can relax. She's alive. And I hope she'll remain alive. But until we take the tube out she won't say a word, so don't get worried."

And at that point the old woman sprang out from nowhere and crossed herself in the direction of the door handle, me and the ceiling. But I didn't get angry with her. I turned and ordered my staff to inject Lidka with camphor and to take turns on duty beside her. Then I went off home across the yard. I remember there was a blue light burning in my study, Döderlein was there, books were lying around. I went over to the couch fully dressed, lay down on it and immediately stopped seeing anything whatsoever; I fell asleep, and didn't even have any dreams.

A month passed, then another. I had already seen a lot of things, and there had already been things more horrific than Lidka's throat. I had forgotten about it. There was snow all around, the numbers at surgery were increasing with every day. And once, already in the New Year, into the surgery came a woman, leading by the hand a little girl, who was wrapped up like a small post. The woman's eyes were shining. I looked closely and recognized her:

"Ah, Lidka! Well, how are things?"

"Everything's fine."

We disentangled Lidka's throat. She was shy and frightened, but I nonetheless managed to lift her chin up and take a look. On her pink neck there was a vertical brown scar and two narrow transverse ones from the stitches.

"Everything's in order," I said, "you don't need to come any more."

"I'm grateful to you, Doctor, thank you," the mother said, and she ordered Lidka: "Say thank you to the man!"

But Lidka didn't want to say anything to me.

Never in my life did I see her again. I started to forget about her. But the numbers coming to my surgery kept on growing. And there came a day when I saw a hundred and ten people. We began at nine o'clock in the morning and finished at eight o'clock in the evening. I was tottering as I took off my gown. The senior midwife-cum-*feldsher* said to me:

"You have the tracheotomy to thank for numbers like this. Do you know what they say in the villages? That you put a steel throat inside sick Lidka in place of her own one, and sewed it in. People travel to her village specially to look at her. There's fame for you, Doctor, congratulations."

"And she continues to live with the steel one?" I enquired.

"She does. And you know, Doctor, you're very good. And the way you're so cool when you do things, it's great."

"Y-yes... You know, I never get worried," I said, without knowing why, but I felt I was too tired even to be

41

embarrassed, I merely looked away. I said goodbye and went off home. Snow was falling heavily, covering everything, the lamp was burning and my house was lonely, quiet and imposing. And as I walked, I wanted only one thing – to sleep.

The Blizzard

Now, just like a beast, it's howling,
Now it cries, just like a child.*

T HE WHOLE STORY BEGAN, according to the omniscient Aksinya, with Palchikov the clerk, who lived in Shalometyevo, falling in love with the agronomist's daughter. The love was ardent, wasting the poor man's heart. He went to Grachovka, the local town, and ordered himself a suit. It turned out to be a dazzling suit, and it's quite possible that it was the grey stripes on his wide, black trousers that decided the unfortunate man's fate. The agronomist's daughter agreed to become his wife.

After removing the leg of a girl who had fallen into a flax breaker, I – the doctor at the hospital of N***, a district of such-and-such a province – became so famous that I almost perished under the weight of my fame. A hundred peasants a day began coming down the smooth sleigh road to my surgery. I stopped eating lunch. Arithmetic is a cruel science. Let's assume that I spent only five minutes on each of my hundred patients... five! Five hundred minutes is eight hours, twenty minutes. On end, note. And on top of that I had an in-patients department for thirty people. And on top of that I did operations too.

In short, returning from the hospital at nine o'clock in the evening, I didn't want to eat, or drink, or sleep. I didn't want anything, apart from nobody coming to call me out to someone in labour. Yet in the course of two weeks I was driven off down the sleigh road during the night half a dozen times.

A dark dampness appeared in my eyes, and a vertical line formed above my nose, like a worm. At night, in a fluctuating mist, I would see unsuccessful operations, ribs laid bare and my hands covered in human blood, and I would wake up sticky and chilly, in spite of the hot tiled stove.

I did my rounds with a swift tread, and behind me swept a male and a female *feldsher* and two nurses. Stopping by a bed on which a patient was melting in a fever and breathing mournfully, I would squeeze out of my brain everything that was held in it. My fingers would grope over his dry, burning skin, I would look at his pupils, tap on his ribs, listen to his heart beating mysteriously in the depths, and I carried within me just the one thought – how was I to save him? And save this one. And this one! All of them.

There was a battle going on. It began every day in the morning, in the pale light of the snow, and it ended in the yellow twinkling of the fervid kerosene lamp.

"How will it end, I'd like to know?" I would say to myself at night. "I mean, they're going to be coming in sledges like this in January, and in February, and in March."

I wrote to Grachovka with a polite reminder of the fact that there was supposed to be a second doctor too in the district of N***.

The letter went forty versts over the even, snowy ocean on a wood-sledge. Three days later came the reply: "Of course, of course," they wrote... "Without fail... only not now... there's no one coming for the moment."

The letter was concluded with some pleasant comments about my work and wishes for further success.

Inspired by these, I started tamponing, injecting diphtheria serum, lancing abscesses of monstrous dimensions, putting on plaster casts...

One Tuesday, not a hundred people came, but a hundred and eleven. I finished the surgery at nine o'clock in the evening. I fell asleep, trying to guess how many there would be tomorrow, on Wednesday. I dreamt that nine hundred people came.

The morning that looked in through the bedroom window was somehow especially white. I opened my eyes, unable to understand what had woken me up. Then I realized – it was a knock.

"Doctor" – I recognized the voice of the midwife, Pelageya Ivanovna – "are you awake?"

"Aha," I replied in a weird voice, only half-awake.

"I've come to tell you not to hurry to the hospital. Only two people have come."

"What? Are you joking?"

"Honestly. There's a blizzard, Doctor, a blizzard," she repeated joyfully through the keyhole. "And the ones who are here have carious teeth. Demyan Lukich will pull them out."

"Surely not…" And I don't know why, but I even leapt out of my bed.

The day turned out splendidly. After doing my rounds, I spent the entire day walking about in my apartment (the quarters allotted to the doctor comprised six rooms, and were for some reason on two floors – three rooms upstairs, and a kitchen and three rooms downstairs), whistling tunes from operas, smoking, drumming on the windows… And going on outside the windows was something I had never seen before. There was no sky, and no earth either. There was whiteness spinning and swirling, hither and thither, back and forth, as though the Devil were playing about with tooth powder.

At noon I gave Aksinya – the acting cook and cleaner for the doctor's apartment – the order to boil up three buckets and one cauldron of water. I hadn't washed for a month.

Aksinya and I extracted from the pantry a trough of unbelievable dimensions. It was set up on the floor in the kitchen. (There could have been no question of a bath in N***sk, of course. There were baths only in the hospital itself – and they were damaged.)

At about two o'clock the spinning web outside the window had thinned out significantly, and I sat naked in the trough with my head covered in lather.

"Now this I can appreciate…" I muttered in delight, splashing the scalding water up onto my back, "this I can appreciate. And after this we'll have lunch, don't you know, and after that we'll fall asleep. And if I get the sleep I need, then let even a hundred and fifty people come tomorrow. What news is there, Aksinya?"

Aksinya was sitting outside the door, waiting for the end of the bathing operation.

"The clerk from the Shalometyevo estate's getting married," replied Aksinya.

"You don't say! She's agreed?"

"Honest to God! He's in lo-ove…" sang Aksinya, making a bit of a clatter with the pots and pans.

"Is the bride pretty?"

"There's none prettier! Blonde, slim…"

"Well I never!…"

And at that moment there was a bang on the door. I gloomily poured water over myself and started to listen hard.

"The doctor's having a bath…" Aksinya was singing out.

"Rumb… rumb…" rumbled a bass voice.

"A note for you, Doctor," squeaked Aksinya through the crack in the door.

"Reach it through the door."

I climbed out of the trough, huddling myself up and indignant with fate, and took from Aksinya's hands a somewhat damp envelope.

"No, not on your life. I'm not going anywhere straight from the trough. After all, I'm human too," I said to myself without much confidence, and opened the note when back in the trough.

Respected colleague [big exclamation mark]. *I impl* [crossed out] *really must ask you to come urgently. After a blow to the head a woman is bleeding from the nasal cav* [crossed out] *from the nose and mouth. Unconscious. I can't manage. I really must ask you to come. The horses are excellent. Her pulse is weak. I've got camphor.*
                                                     Dr [signature illegible].

"I have no luck in life," I thought dolefully, gazing at the hot firewood in the stove.

"Was the note brought by a man?"

"It was."

"Let him come in here."

He came in, and to me he looked like an ancient Roman, because of the brilliant helmet he wore over the top of his big-eared hat. He was enveloped in a wolf-skin coat, and I was struck by a current of cold.

"Why are you wearing a helmet?" I asked, covering my partially washed body with a sheet.

"I'm a fireman from Shalometyevo. We've got a fire brigade there..." replied the Roman.

"Who's this doctor that's writing?"

"He came to visit our agronomist. A young doctor. What a misfortune we've had, oh what a misfortune..."

"Who's the woman?"

"The clerk's fiancée."

Outside the door Aksinya gave a groan.

"What happened?" (Aksinya's body could be heard pressing up against the door.)

47

"It was the betrothal yesterday, and after the betrothal the clerk wanted to take her for a sleigh ride. He harnessed up a trotting horse, sat her in the sleigh, and out through the gate. But the horse tore off and his fiancée gave a lurch and hit her forehead on the gatepost. And that's how she came to fly out. Such a misfortune that words can't express it… The clerk's being followed so that he doesn't hang himself. He's lost his senses."

"I'm having a bath," I said plaintively, "why on earth didn't you bring her here?" And at the same time I poured water over my head, and the soap went into the trough.

"Unthinkable, respected Citizen Doctor," said the fireman with feeling, and he clasped his hands together as if in prayer, "not a chance. The girl will die."

"But how are we to get there? The blizzard!"

"It's died down. Do come, sir. It's completely died down. They're fast horses, harnessed in single file. We'll fly there in an hour…"

I groaned meekly and climbed out of the trough. Poured two bucketfuls over myself in a frenzy. Then, squatting down before the jaws of the stove, I poked my head into them to dry off, even if only a little.

"I'll end up with pneumonia, of course. Lobar pneumonia, after such a journey. And the main thing is, what am I going to do with her? It's clear from the note alone that this doctor is even less experienced than I am. I don't know anything. In six months I've just picked a bit up from practice, and he knows even less. He's evidently just left university. And he takes me for someone with experience…"

Reflecting thus, I didn't even notice that I had got dressed. Getting dressed wasn't easy: trousers and a blouse, felt boots, over the blouse a leather jacket, then an overcoat, and a sheepskin coat on top, a hat, a bag, and in it caffeine, camphor, morphine, adrenalin, torsion forceps, sterile cloth, a syringe, a probe, a Browning, cigarettes, matches, a watch, a stethoscope.

It didn't seem at all frightening, although it was getting dark and the day was already melting away as we drove out of the village. It was apparently snowing a little more lightly. It was slanting down, in one direction, into my right cheek. The mountain of the fireman shielded me from the crupper of the first horse. The horses did, indeed, set to briskly, they stretched out, and the sledge went flying over the bumpy road. I lay down in the sledge, got warm straight away, and thought about lobar pneumonia, and about how the girl's cranial bone had possibly cracked from within and a splinter pierced the brain…

"Are they fire-brigade horses?" I asked through my sheep-skin collar.

"Oowhoo… whoo…" rumbled my driver, without turning round.

"And what did the doctor do to her?"

"Oh, he… whoo, whoo… he studied venereal diseases, you see… oowhoo… whoo…"

"Whoo… whoo…" the blizzard started thundering in a copse, and then, from the side and with a whistle, down it sprinkled… I began to be rocked to sleep, I was rocked and rocked… until I found myself in the Sandunovsky Baths in Moscow. And I was still in my fur coat, in the changing room, and covered in perspiration. Then a torch flared up, the cold was let in, I opened my eyes and saw a bloody helmet gleaming, thought there was a fire… and then came to, and realized I had arrived. I was by the threshold of a white building with columns, apparently of the time of Nicholas I.* There was deep darkness all around, but I was met by firemen, and there was flame dancing above their heads. Straight away I extracted my watch from a slit in my fur coat and saw that it was five. So we had been travelling for not one, but two and a half hours.

"Let me have horses to go back at once," I said.

"Yes, sir," replied my driver.

Half-asleep, and wet under my leather jacket as if in a compress, I went into the lobby. I was struck from one side by the light of a lamp, and a strip of it fell onto the painted floor. And at this point a fair-haired young man with haunted eyes came running out, wearing trousers with a freshly pressed crease in them. His white tie with black spots was twisted to one side, his shirt front had popped out like a hump, but his jacket was spick and span, new, and with such creases, they seemed to be metallic.

The man waved his arms, seized hold of my fur coat, gave me a shake, clung on to me and began crying out very quietly:

"My dear... Doctor... quickly... she's dying. I'm a murderer." He looked off to the side somewhere, closed his eyes sternly and blackly, and said to someone or other: "I'm a murderer, that's what I am."

Then he started sobbing, grabbed at his straggly hair and tugged on it, and I saw that he genuinely was tearing at his locks, winding them around his fingers.

"Stop," I said to him, and gave his arm a squeeze.

Somebody drew him away. Some women came running out.

Someone took my fur coat off me, and I was led over rugs put down for the celebration and brought to a white bed. The young doctor rose from a chair to meet me. His eyes were tormented and bewildered. For an instant there was a glimpse of surprise in them that I was just as young as he himself. All in all we were like two portraits of one and the same person, and of the same age. But then he was so pleased to see me that he even choked.

"How glad I am... colleague... now... her pulse is failing, you see. I'm actually a venereologist. I'm terribly glad you've come."

On a scrap of gauze on the table lay a syringe and several ampoules of yellow oil. From outside the door came the clerk's crying, then the door was pushed to and the figure of a woman in white appeared at my shoulder. There was semi-darkness in the bedroom, the lamp had a scrap of green cloth hanging down over one side of it. On the pillow in the greenish shade lay a face the colour of paper. Locks of fair hair were drooping down and scattered about. The nose had sharpened, and the nostrils were stuffed with cotton wool that was pinkish with blood.

"Her pulse..." the doctor whispered to me.

I took hold of the lifeless hand, applied my fingers with what was already a customary gesture, and winced. Beneath my fingers there began a shallow, frequent trembling, then it started to be broken, stretched to a thread. I felt the customary cold in the pit of my stomach, as I always did when I saw death close to. I hate death. I managed to break off the end of an ampoule and draw the thick oil into my syringe. But it was already mechanically that I injected it, and I squeezed it in under the skin of the maidenly arm for nothing.

The girl's lower jaw began to jerk as if she were choking, then it sagged, and her body tensed underneath the blanket, seemed to freeze, then went slack. And the last thread disappeared beneath my fingers.

"She's dead," I said into the doctor's ear.

The white figure with grey hair dropped onto the smooth blanket, pressed against it and started to shake.

"Steady now, steady," I said into the woman in white's ear, while the doctor cast a sidelong look full of suffering at the door.

"I can't take any more of him," said the doctor very quietly.

This is what we did: we left the crying woman in the bedroom, said nothing to anyone and led the clerk away into a distant room.

There I said to him:

"If you don't allow yourself to be injected with some medicine, we can do nothing. You're wearing us out, hindering our work!"

At that point he consented; crying quietly, he took off his jacket, we rolled back the sleeve of the smart shirt he was in as the fiancé, and injected him with morphine. The doctor went off to the dead woman, ostensibly to help her, while I lingered beside the clerk. The morphine helped more quickly than I had expected. After a quarter of an hour, crying and complaining ever more quietly and incoherently, the clerk began to drop off, then laid his tear-stained face down on his arms and fell asleep. He didn't hear the commotion, the crying, the rustling or the muffled wails.

"Listen, colleague, it's dangerous to travel. You might get lost," the doctor said to me in a whisper in the entrance hall. "Stay here, stay the night…"

"No, I can't. I'm leaving, come what may. I was promised that I'd be taken back straight away."

"And you will, only be warned…"

"I've got three patients with typhus that I can't leave on their own. I have to see them during the night."

"Well, but be warned…"

He diluted some alcohol with water and gave it to me to drink, and there in the entrance hall I ate a piece of ham. My stomach grew warm, and the anguish in my heart shrank a little. I went into the bedroom one last time and looked at the dead woman, popped in to see the clerk, left the doctor an ampoule of morphine and went out onto the porch all wrapped up.

There the storm was whistling, the horses had hung their heads and the snow was lashing them. A torch was being tossed about.

"Do you know the way?" I asked, covering up my mouth.

"We know the way," replied the driver very sadly (he was no longer wearing the helmet), "but you ought to stay the night..."

Even by the ears of his hat you could see that he would almost rather die than go.

"You should stay," added another man who was holding the frenzied torch, "it's bad out in the fields, sir."

"Twelve versts," I rumbled morosely, "we'll get there. I've got seriously ill patients..." and I climbed into the sledge.

I confess I didn't add that just the very thought of staying in that wing, where there was woe and where I was powerless and useless, seemed to me unbearable.

The driver flopped down hopelessly onto his seat, straightened up, swayed, and we leapt out through the gates. The torch vanished as though the earth had swallowed it up, or else it had gone out. A minute later, however, something else grabbed my interest. Turning around with difficulty, I saw that not only was there no torch, but Shalometyevo and all its buildings had disappeared, as if in a dream. This stung me in an unpleasant way.

"This is great, though..." I either thought, or muttered. I poked my nose out for a moment, then hid it again, things were so nasty. The whole world had curled itself up into a ball, and it was being pulled about in all directions.

The thought popped into my head that perhaps we should go back? But I suppressed it, sank down deeper into the hay on the bottom of the sledge as though into a boat, huddled myself up and closed my eyes. Straight away there swam up the scrap of cloth on the lamp and the white face. My mind suddenly cleared: "It was a fracture of the base of the skull. Yes, yes, yes... Aha, aha... exactly so!" Certainty that this was the correct diagnosis blazed out. It had dawned on me. Well, and what was the use? It was no use now, and nor would it have been of any use before. What could you have done with it? What a terrible fate! How absurd and terrifying it is to live on earth! What would happen now in the agronomist's house? Even thinking of it makes you feel sick and miserable! Then I began feeling sorry for myself: what a hard life I have. People are asleep now, their stoves are well heated, but I have again been unable even to have a wash. I am being borne by the blizzard like a leaf. Right then, I'll get home, and who knows, I might be taken off somewhere again. I'll just carry on flying through the blizzard. There's one of me, but there are thousands of patients... I'll go and get pneumonia and die here myself... And so, having moved myself to pity, I plunged down into darkness, but how long I was there I don't know. I didn't find myself in any bath-houses, and I began to feel cold. And ever colder and colder.

When I opened my eyes, I saw a black back, and only after that did I grasp that we weren't moving, but standing still.

"Are we there?" I asked, goggling dully.

The black driver stirred mournfully and suddenly dismounted, and it seemed to me as if he was being spun in all directions... and he spoke without any deference:

"Oh, we're there all right... You ought to have listened to people... I mean, you see what happens! We're going to kill both ourselves and the horses..."

"We haven't lost the road, have we?" My spine turned cold.

"What road's that?" the driver responded in a downcast voice. "The whole wide world's our road now... We're done for, and all in vain... We've been driving for four hours, but where to... I mean, you see what's going on..."

For four hours. I started groping about, found my watch, took out my matches. Why? There was no use in it, not one single match produced a flame. You'd strike one, there'd be a flash – and the light would instantly be lost without trace.

"About four hours, I'm telling you," said the fireman funereally. "Now what do we do?"

"Where are we now?"

The question was so stupid that the driver didn't consider it necessary to answer it. He was turning in various directions, but it seemed to me at times that he was standing still, while I was being spun about in the sledge. I clambered out and immediately found that the snow by the runner came up to my knee. The rear horse was stuck belly-deep in a snowdrift. Its mane was hanging down like a woman's loosened hair.

"Did they stop by themselves?"

"By themselves. The animals have had enough..."

I suddenly remembered certain stories, and for some reason felt anger towards Leo Tolstoy.

"It was all right for him at Yasnaya Polyana,"* I thought, "I don't suppose *he* was taken to see people who were dying..."

I began to feel sorry for the fireman and for myself. Then I experienced a flash of wild terror again. But I crushed it in my breast.

"That's... faint-heartedness..." I muttered through my teeth.

And impetuous energy surged up inside me.

"Here's what, dad," I began, sensing that my teeth were freezing, "we mustn't give in to despondency now, or else we really will go to the devil. They've stopped for a bit, had a rest, now we have to move on. You walk, take the horse at the front by the bridle, and I'll drive. We have to get out of this, or else we'll be snowed in."

The ears of his hat looked desperate, but the driver moved forwards all the same. Plodding along and sinking down, he made his way to the first horse. It seemed to me to take an endlessly long time to get out. The figure of the driver became blurred to my eyes, they had the dry snow of the blizzard driven into them.

"Gee-ee up," moaned the driver.

"Gee up! Gee up!" I cried, cracking the reins.

Little by little the horses moved off and started wading through the snow. The sledge rocked as if on a wave. The driver now grew taller, now became smaller as he tried to find a way out in front.

We moved like this for about a quarter of an hour, until I finally sensed that the sledge seemed to have started crunching along more evenly. Joy surged into me when I began to see glimpses of a horse's rear hooves.

"It's not deep here, this is a road!" I cried.

"Oho... Oho..." the driver responded. He plodded back to me and immediately grew taller.

"It does seem to be a road," the fireman responded joyfully, even with a trill in his voice. "As long as we don't stray again... Maybe..."

We changed our seats. The horses set off more vigorously. The blizzard was definitely abating, it had begun to weaken, or so it seemed to me. But above and to the sides there was nothing but murk. I no longer hoped to arrive specifically at the hospital. I just wanted to arrive *somewhere*. After all, roads lead to dwelling places.

The horses suddenly gave a jerk and began working their legs with greater vigour. I rejoiced, as I didn't yet know the reason for it.

"Have they, maybe, sensed some dwelling?" I asked.

The driver didn't answer me. I lifted myself up a little in the sledge and started peering out. A strange sound arose, mournful and malicious, somewhere in the gloom, but quickly died away. I had an unpleasant feeling for some reason, and I recalled the clerk and the way he had whined thinly, with his head laid on his arms. Suddenly I made out a dark dot on the right-hand side, and it grew into a black cat, and then grew some more and came closer. The fireman suddenly turned round to me, at which point I saw that his jaw was jumping, and he asked:

"Did you see, Citizen Doctor?"

One horse flung itself to the right, the other to the left, the fireman fell back onto my lap for a second, groaned, straightened up, and then began, supporting himself, yanking on the reins. The horses snorted and bolted. They were throwing the snow up in clods, tossing it about, moving unevenly, trembling.

And a tremor ran through my body several times too. Recovering myself, I put my hand inside my bosom, took out my Browning and cursed myself for having left the second cartridge clip at home. No, if I hadn't stayed for the night, then why hadn't I brought a torch with me?! In my mind I saw a short announcement in the newspaper about me and the ill-starred fireman.

The cat had grown into a dog and started bowling along not far from the sledge. I turned around and saw very close behind the sledge a second four-legged creature. I can swear that it had pointed ears and was moving easily behind the sledge, as if on a parquet floor. There was something menacing and insolent in its speed. "A pack, or just the two of them?" I wondered, and at the word "pack" I was thrown into a cold sweat beneath my fur coat and my toes stopped freezing.

"Hold on tight, and hold back the horses," I said in a voice not my own, unknown to me.

The driver only groaned in reply and drew his head into his shoulders. There was a flash in my eyes and a deafening bang. Then for a second time and a third. I don't remember for how many minutes I was bumped about on the bottom of the sledge. I listened to the wild, shrill snorting of the horses, squeezed the Browning, hit my head on something, tried to emerge out of the hay, and thought in mortal terror that an enormous, wiry body was suddenly going to appear on my chest. In my mind I already saw my ripped intestines...

At that moment the driver howled:

"Oho... oho... there it is... there... Lord, preserve me, preserve me..."

I finally got the better of my heavy sheepskin, freed my arms and lifted myself up. There were no black beasts either behind or to the sides. The swirling snow was light and tolerable, and glimmering in the light shroud was the most enchanting eye, which I would have known in a thousand, which I know even now – it was the glimmering of my hospital's lamp. Something dark loomed behind it. "Far more beautiful than a palace..." I reflected, and suddenly, in ecstasy, I fired two more bullets from the Browning, backwards, towards where the wolves had disappeared.

The fireman stood in the middle of the stairs leading from the lower section of the splendid doctor's apartment, I at the top of those stairs, Aksinya in a sheepskin coat at the bottom.

"Load me with money," began my driver, "if ever again I..." He didn't finish what he was saying, knocked back his diluted spirit in one, let out a dreadful croak, turned to Aksinya and added, spreading his arms wide, as far as his build allowed: "This big..."

"Is she dead? You didn't save her?" Aksinya asked me.

"She's dead," I answered indifferently.

A quarter of an hour later it was quiet. The light had gone out downstairs. I remained alone upstairs. For some reason I gave a spasmodic grin, undid the buttons of my blouse, then did them up, went to the bookshelf, took out a volume on surgery, wanted to look at something about fractures of the base of the skull, but put the book down.

When I had undressed and got under the blanket, I was shaken by tremors for about half a minute, but then they eased, and warmth spread all through my body.

"Load me with money," I rumbled, beginning to doze off, "but no more will I..."

"You will go... actually, you will..." the blizzard started whistling mockingly. It went thundering across the roof. Then it sang in the chimney, flew out of it, rustled outside the window and disappeared.

"Yes you will go... yes you will go..." ticked the clock, but more and more indistinctly.

And then nothing. Silence. Sleep.

Egyptian Darkness*

WHERE EVER IS ALL the world on my birthday? Where are the electric street lamps of Moscow? The people? The sky? Outside the windows there is nothing! Darkness...

We are cut off from people. The first kerosene lamps are nine versts away from us at the railway station. There's probably a lamp twinkling there, breathing its last because of the snowstorm. The fast train to Moscow will go howling by at midnight and won't even stop – it has no need of a forgotten station, buried in a blizzard. Unless the tracks are snowed under.

The first electric street lamps are forty versts away in the local town. Life there is sweet. There's a cinematograph, shops. At the same time as it's howling and the snow's coming down hard on the fields, on the screen there may be floating reeds, swaying palms, a twinkling tropical island.

But we're alone.

"Egyptian darkness," remarked Demyan Lukich, the *feldsher*, raising the blind a little.

He expresses himself grandly, but very accurately. Precisely – Egyptian.

"Do have another glass," I suggested. (Ah, don't be critical! I mean, a doctor, a *feldsher*, two midwives, we're human too, after all! We see no one for months on end, apart from hundreds of patients. We work, we're buried in snow. Are we really not allowed to drink two glasses of spirit, diluted as prescribed, accompanied by a snack of sprats from the local town on the doctor's birthday?)

"Good health, Doctor!" said Demyan Lukich with feeling.

"We hope you get used to being here with us!" said Anna Nikolayevna, and clinking glasses, she straightened her best, patterned dress.

The second midwife, Pelageya Ivanovna, clinked glasses, gulped down her drink, and immediately squatted down and moved the poker around in the stove. A hot glow was cast across our faces, and the vodka was making it warm inside our chests.

"I simply can't believe," I began excitedly, looking at the cloud of sparks that flew up from beneath the poker, "what that woman did with the belladonna. I mean, it's just a nightmare!"

Smiles began to play on the faces of the *feldsher* and the midwives.

This is what it was all about. That morning during morning surgery, pushing her way into my room had come a rosy peasant woman of about thirty. She had bowed towards the obstetric chair standing behind my back, then taken a wide-necked flask from her bosom and begun to pipe flatteringly:

"Thank you for the drops, Citizen Doctor. They helped me ever such a lot, ever such a lot!... Let me have another jar."

I had taken the flask from her hands, glanced at the label, and everything had gone into a spin before my eyes. Written on the label in Demyan Lukich's bold hand was: "Tinct. belladonna..." etc. "16th December 1917".

In other words, yesterday I had prescribed the woman a respectable dose of belladonna, and today, on my birthday, the 17th of December, the woman had come to me with a dry flask and a request to repeat the prescription.

"Did you... did you... take it all yesterday?" I had asked in a wild voice.

"All of it, kind sir, all of it," the woman had piped in a sugary tone. "God grant you good health for those drops...

half a jar when I got home, and half a jar when it was time for bed. I felt better in a trice…"

I had leant against the obstetric chair.

"How many drops at a time did I tell you?" I had said in a strangled voice. "I said five drops at a time… What are you doing, woman? You… I…"

"Honest to God, I did take them!" the woman had said, thinking I didn't believe her when she said she'd treated herself with my belladonna.

I had grasped her rosy cheeks in my hands and begun peering into her pupils. But there had been nothing wrong with her pupils. Quite pretty, perfectly normal. The woman's pulse had been splendid too. All in all, the woman had shown no signs of belladonna poisoning.

"It can't be!…" I had said, and yelled: "Demyan Lukich!"

Demyan Lukich in a white coat had appeared from the pharmacy corridor.

"Demyan Lukich, just look what this beauty has done! I don't understand a thing…"

The woman had spun her head from side to side in fright, realizing she had done something wrong.

Demyan Lukich had seized the flask, sniffed at it, turned it over in his hands and said sternly:

"You're lying, my dear. You didn't take the medicine!"

"Honest to…" the woman had begun.

"Don't try pulling the wool over our eyes, woman," Demyan Lukich had said with a twist of his mouth, "we fully understand everything. Confess it, who have you been treating with these drops?"

The woman had raised her normal pupils to the clean, whitewashed ceiling and crossed herself.

"May I be…"

"Stop it, stop it…" Demyan Lukich had grumbled, and then turned to me: "Here's what they do, you know, Doctor.

An actress like this will come to the hospital, she'll be prescribed some medicine, and she'll go back to her village and give some to all of the women..."

"What are you saying, Citizen Fershel..."

"Stop it!" the *feldsher* had snapped. "I've been seeing you for eight years. I know. Of course she used up the whole flask, giving drops to every household," he had continued to me.

"Give me some more of those drops," the woman had pleaded.

"Oh no, woman," I had replied, wiping the sweat from my brow, "you won't be getting any more treatment with those drops. Is your stomach better?"

"I seemed to be, well, better in a trice!..."

"Well, that's excellent. I'll prescribe some different ones for you, they're very good too."

And I had prescribed the woman valerian drops, and she had left disappointed.

This was the incident of which we talked in my doctor's apartment on my birthday, while outside the windows there hung, like a heavy curtain, the Egyptian darkness of the snowstorm.

"This is the thing," said Demyan Lukich, chewing the fish in oil with delicacy, "this is the thing: we've already got used to it here. Whereas you, dear Doctor, after university, after the capital, you'll have to work very, very hard at getting used to it. It's the backwoods!"

"Oh, the real backwoods too!" responded Anna Nikolayevna like an echo.

The snowstorm began howling somewhere in the flues, and rustled on the other side of the wall. A reflected crimson glow settled on the dark sheet of iron by the stove. A blessing on the fire that warms medical personnel in the backwoods!

"Have you heard about your predecessor, Leopold Leopoldovich?" said the *feldsher*, and after delicately helping Anna Nikolayevna to a cigarette, he lit one for himself.

"He was a marvellous doctor!" said Pelageya Ivanna enthusiastically, peering into the blessed fire with shining eyes. Her best comb with its fake stones would flare up and die away in her black hair.

"Yes, an outstanding person," the *feldsher* confirmed. "The peasants simply adored him. He had the right approach with them. Come to Liponty for an operation – by all means! Instead of Leopold Leopoldovich they called him Liponty Lipontyevich. They trusted him. Well, and he knew how to talk to them. Well and so, then, a friend of his comes to see him once, Fyodor Kosoy from Dultsevo, he comes to surgery. And he goes, 'Liponty Lipontyich,' he says, 'my chest's all congested, well, I can't breathe freely. And apart from that, it's as if there's a scratching in my throat.'"

"Laryngitis," I said mechanically, having already grown accustomed in a month of frenzied haste to the lightning diagnoses of the countryside.

"Perfectly correct. 'Well,' says Liponty, 'I'll give you something for it. You'll be well in two days. Here are some mustard plasters for you from France. You'll stick one on your back between your wings, another on your chest. You'll keep them on for ten minutes, then take them off. Quick march! Action!' So he took the mustard plasters and left. Two days later he appears at surgery.

"'What's the matter?' asks Liponty.

"And Kosoy says to him:

"'Well,' he says, 'Liponty Lipontyich, your mustard plasters are no help.'

"'What rubbish you do talk!' replies Liponty, 'mustard plasters from France can't fail to help! I suppose you didn't put them on?'

"'What do you mean,' he says, 'didn't put them on? They're on even now...'

"And at that he turns his back, and he's got a mustard plaster stuck on his sheepskin coat!..."

I burst into loud laughter, while Pelageya Ivanna began giggling and banged the poker fiercely on a log.

"Say what you like, that's a joke," I said, "it can't be true."

"A joke?! A joke?!" the midwives exclaimed, both at the same time.

"No, sir!" the *feldsher* exclaimed fiercely. "Our whole life, you know, is made up of jokes like that... That's the sort of thing we have happening here..."

"What about the sugar?!" exclaimed Anna Nikolayevna. "Tell him about the sugar, Pelageya Ivanna!"

Pelageya Ivanna closed the stove door and, looking down at the floor, began:

"I go to that same Dultsevo to a woman in labour—"

"That Dultsevo's a renowned place," said the *feldsher*, unable to restrain himself, adding: "Sorry! Continue, colleague!"

"Well, naturally, I carry out an examination," his colleague Pelageya Ivanna continued, "and inside the birth canal I can feel something under my fingers that I can't understand... One moment it's free-flowing, the next it's in chunks... it turns out to be lump sugar!"

"Now there's a joke!" remarked Demyan Lukich triumphantly.

"For-give me... I don't understand a thing..."

"An old woman!" Pelageya Ivanna responded. "A wise woman taught her. She's having a difficult labour, she says. The baby doesn't want to come out into the big wide world. And so it needs to be lured out. So there they were, luring it out with something sweet!"

"'That's awful!" I said.

66

"They give women hair to chew when they're in labour," said Anna Nikolayevna.

"Why?!"

"Goodness knows. They've been brought to us two or three times, and the poor woman's lying there spitting. Her whole mouth is full of bristles. There's this belief that it'll be an easier labour..."

The midwives' eyes had started sparkling at the memories. We sat by the fire with our tea for a long time, and I listened spellbound. About how, when a woman in labour has to be brought to us at the hospital from her village, Pelageya Ivanna always sets off in her sledge behind, in case they change their minds on the way and take the mother-to-be back to the hands of a wise woman. About how once, when a woman was giving birth to a child that was lying incorrectly, they suspended her from the ceiling with her legs uppermost to make the baby turn. About how, having heard a lot about the way doctors puncture the birth sac, a wise woman from Korobovo cut the whole of a baby's head to pieces with a kitchen knife, so that even a man as renowned and skilful as Liponty was unable to save it, and did well even to save the mother. About how...

The stove had been shut long ago. My guests had left for their wing. I saw a dimmish light shining for a time at Anna Nikolayevna's little window, before going out. Everything vanished. Added to the snowstorm was the dense dark of the December evening, and both heaven and earth were hidden from me by a black curtain.

I paced up and down my study, and the floor creaked beneath my feet, and the tiled stove made it warm, and somewhere a busy mouse could be heard gnawing...

"No," I pondered, "I shall struggle against Egyptian darkness for just as long as Fate keeps me here in the backwoods. Lump sugar... For goodness' sake!..."

In the reverie born in the light of the lamp under its green shade there arose a huge university city, and in it a clinic, and in the clinic a huge hall, a tiled floor, shiny taps, white, sterile sheets, a junior teacher with a little, pointed, very wise, greying beard...

A knock at such moments is always disturbing, frightening. I gave a start...

"Who is it, Aksinya?" I asked, hanging over the balustrade of the indoor staircase (the doctor's apartment was on two floors: upstairs a study and a bedroom, and downstairs a dining room, another room of unknown purpose and the kitchen, in which were housed this Aksinya, the cook, and her husband, the hospital's permanent watchman).

The heavy bolt rattled, the light of a lamp began moving and swaying downstairs, there was a breath of cold air. Then Aksinya announced:

"There's a sick man here..."

To tell the truth, I was glad. I didn't feel sleepy yet, and the gnawing of the mouse and my memories had made me a little melancholy and lonely. And a sick *man*, what's more, so not a woman, so not the most terrifying thing – not childbirth.

"Can he walk?"

"He can," replied Aksinya, yawning.

"Well, let him come into the study."

The staircase creaked for a long time. It was somebody sizable coming up, a man of great weight. I was already sitting at the desk now, trying, as far as possible, not to let my twenty-four-year-old vigour leap out of the professional Aesculapian shell. My right hand lay on my stethoscope as if it were a revolver.

In through the door squeezed a figure in a sheepskin coat and felt boots. In the figure's hands was a hat.

"What on earth are you doing here so late, old fellow?" I asked seriously, to clear my conscience.

68

"I'm sorry, Citizen Doctor," the figure responded in a pleasant, soft bass voice, "it's the snowstorm – it's an utter nuisance! Well, we were delayed, but what can you do; please, do forgive me!"

"A polite man," I thought with pleasure. I liked the figure very much, and even his thick red beard made a good impression. This beard evidently enjoyed a certain amount of care. Not only had its owner trimmed it, he had even lubricated it with some substance which a doctor who had spent even only a short period in the country had no difficulty in recognizing as vegetable oil.

"What's the matter? Take your coat off. Where are you from?"

The coat fell in a heap onto a chair.

"The fever's driving me mad," the sick man replied, giving me a doleful look.

"Fever? Aha! Are you from Dultsevo?"

"Yes, sir. I'm the miller."

"Well, and how does it drive you mad? Tell me!"

"Every day, as soon as it's twelve o'clock, my head starts aching, then the fever starts... I'm feverish for a couple of hours, then it eases."

"The diagnosis is ready!" resounded triumphantly in my head.

"And you're all right the rest of the time?"

"My legs are weak..."

"Aha... Undo your things! Hm... right."

By the end of the examination the sick man had enchanted me. After slow-witted old women and frightened adolescents who recoiled in horror from a metal spatula, after that morning's trick with the belladonna, the miller was restful for my university eye.

The miller's speech was sensible. Besides that, he proved to be literate, and even his every gesture was imbued

69

with respect for the science that I consider my best loved
– medicine.

"Do you know what, my dear fellow," I said, tapping
his immensely broad, warm chest, "you've got malaria.
Intermittent fever... I've got a whole ward free at the moment. I very much advise you to stay here with me. We'll
keep you under proper observation. I'll start treating you
with powders, and if that doesn't help, we'll give you some
injections. We'll have a successful outcome. Eh? Will you
stay?..."

"I'm most humbly grateful to you!" the miller replied
very politely. "I've heard a lot about you. Everyone's satisfied. They say you help them so much. And I consent to the
injections, if only I can recover."

"No, this is one truly bright ray in the darkness!" I thought,
and sat down at the desk to write.

The feeling I had as I did was so pleasant, it was as though
not a strange miller, but my own brother had come to stay
at the hospital.

On one prescription form I wrote:

Chinini mur. 0.5
D.T. dos. No. 10
S. Miller Khudov
1 powder at midnight.

And added a flamboyant signature.
And on another form:

Pelageya Ivanovna! Admit the miller to ward 2. He has
malaria. One quinine powder, as required, some 4 hours
before an attack, that is, at midnight.
*   Here's an exception for you! A cultured miller!*

I was already lying in bed when I received a note in reply from the hands of the sullen and yawning Aksinya:

Dear Doctor! I've done everything.
                                    Pel. Lbova.

And I fell asleep.

...And woke up.

"What is it? What? What, Aksinya?!" I mumbled.

Aksinya stood covering herself bashfully with a skirt patterned with white dots on a dark background.

A flickering stearin candle lit up her sleepy, anxious face.

"Maria just came running, Pelageya Ivanovna said you were to be called straight away."

"What's the matter?"

"She says the miller in ward two is dying."

"Wha-at?! Dying? How can he be dying?!"

My bare feet, missing my slippers, instantly sensed the cool floor. I spent a long time breaking matches and poking them into the burner before it lit with a bluish flame. By the clock it was exactly six.

"What's the matter?... What's the matter? Surely it isn't something other than malaria? What ever is the matter with him? His pulse is fine..."

No more than five minutes later, in socks I had put on inside out, in an unbuttoned jacket, with tousled hair, in felt boots, I slipped across the yard, which was still completely dark, and went running into ward two.

On a bed without covers, beside a crumpled sheet, wearing just his hospital linen, sat the miller. He was lit by a small kerosene lamp. His red beard was tousled, and his eyes appeared to me black and huge. He was rocking slightly, like a drunk. Gazing around in horror, breathing heavily...

71

Maria the nurse was looking open-mouthed at his dark-crimson face.

Pelageya Ivanovna, bareheaded and with her white coat awry, rushed to meet me.

"Doctor!" she exclaimed in a rather hoarse voice, "I swear to you, it's not my fault! Who ever could have expected it? You said it yourself – cultured..."

"What's wrong?"

Pelageya Ivanovna clasped her hands and said:

"Just imagine, Doctor! He took all ten quinine powders at once! At midnight."

It was a rather murky winter's dawn. Demyan Lukich was clearing away the stomach pump. There was a smell of camphor oil. The basin on the floor was full of a brownish liquid. The miller was lying exhausted and pale, covered up to the chin with a white sheet. His red beard was sticking up on end. Bending down, I felt his pulse, and was satisfied that the miller had pulled through all right.

"Well, how do you feel?"

"I've got Egyptian darkness in front of my eyes... Oh... o-oh..." the miller responded in a weak voice.

"So have I!" I replied irritably.

"Huh?" the miller responded (he still couldn't hear very well).

"Explain just one thing to me, dad: why did you do that?!" I shouted into his ear a little louder.

And a gloomy, hostile bass responded:

"Why hang around here with you, I thought, taking one little powder at a time? I took them all at once, and that was the end of the matter."

"That's monstrous!" I exclaimed.

"A joke!" responded the *feldsher*, as though distracted, but caustically.

* * *

"But no… I'm going to struggle. I'm going to… I'm…" And after a difficult night, sweet sleep enveloped me. A shroud of Egyptian darkness stretched out… and it was as if I were in it… with either a sword or a stethoscope. And on I went… Struggling… In the backwoods. But not alone. Onwards went my host: Demyan Lukich, Anna Nikolayevna, Pelageya Ivanovna. All in white coats, and ever onwards, onwards…

It's a good thing, sleep!…

The Starry Rash

THIS IS IT! It was my instinct that told me. It was no use counting on my knowledge. A doctor who had graduated from university just six months before, I, of course, had no knowledge.

I was afraid to touch the man's bare, warm shoulder (although there was no reason to be afraid), and ordered him verbally:

"Come on, Dad, move closer to the light!"

The man turned as I wanted him to, and the light of the kerosene lamp flooded his yellowish skin. Showing through this yellowness on his bulging chest and on his sides was a marmoreal rash. "Like the stars in the sky," I thought, and with a chill in my stomach I leant towards his chest, then took my eyes off it and lifted them to his face. The face before me was forty years old, wearing a tangled little beard of a dirty ashen colour, with lively little eyes concealed by swollen lids. In those eyes, to my great surprise, I read self-importance and a sense of personal dignity.

The man was blinking and looking around in indifference and boredom, adjusting the belt on his trousers.

"This is it – syphilis," I said sternly in my mind for a second time. This was the first time in my medical life I had come across it, I, a doctor tossed straight from university into the depths of the countryside at the start of the Revolution.

I had come across this case of syphilis by chance. The man had come to see me, complaining that his throat was blocked. Quite inexplicably, and without thinking of syphilis, I had told him to undress, and it was then that I had seen this starry rash.

I put together the hoarseness, the ominous redness in his throat, the strange white spots in it, the marmoreal chest, and I guessed. First of all I faint-heartedly rubbed my hands with a ball of mercuric chloride, while the anxious thought "I think he coughed on my hands" poisoned the minute for me. Then helplessly and squeamishly I turned in my hands the glass spatula that I had used to examine my patient's throat. Where was I to put it?

I decided to lay it on the window sill, on a ball of cotton wool.

"The thing is," I said, "you see… Hm… Seemingly… Actually, even for sure… You see, you've got a bad disease – syphilis…"

I said this, and then became confused. I had thought that the man would be very frightened, would get very upset…

He didn't get upset at all and wasn't frightened. He looked at me askance, from the side somehow, like the way a chicken looks with one round eye when it hears a voice calling it. In this round eye, to my great amazement, I noted mistrust.

"You've got syphilis," I repeated softly.

"And what's that?" asked the man with the marmoreal rash.

At this point there flashed vividly before my eyes the edge of a snow-white ward, a university ward, an amphitheatre with students' heads piled up on top of one another, and the grey beard of a professor specializing in venereal diseases… But I quickly came to and remembered that I was fifteen hundred versts from the amphitheatre and forty versts from the railway, in the light of a kerosene lamp… Beyond the white door was the muffled noise of the numerous patients waiting their turn. Outside the window twilight was steadily falling, and the first snow of winter was flying.

I made the patient undress still more and found the primary lesion, which was already healing. My last doubts left me, and I was visited by the feeling of pride which was invariably there every time I made a correct diagnosis.

"Do yourself up," I began, "you've got syphilis! A very serious disease which takes hold of the entire organism. You'll need to have lengthy treatment!..."

At this point I hesitated because – I swear it! – I read in that gaze like a chicken's a surprise that was obviously mixed with irony.

"My throat's gone and got hoarse," said the patient.

"Well, yes, and that's what's made it get hoarse. And that's why you've got the rash on your chest. Look at your chest..."

The man squinted and had a look. The ironic light in his eyes didn't go out.

"I could do with some treatment for my throat," he said.

"Why does he keep on about what *he* thinks?" I thought, already with a certain impatience. "I talk about syphilis, and he talks about his throat!"

"Listen, Dad," I continued out loud, "your throat is a secondary matter. We'll help your throat too, but the main thing is that your illness as a whole needs treatment. And you'll need to have treatment over a long time – two years."

At this point the patient goggled at me. And in his eyes I read his verdict on me: "You're off your head, Doctor!"

"Why so long?" asked the patient. "How can that be, two years?! I could do with some kind of gargle for my throat..."

Everything blazed up inside me. And I began talking. I was no longer afraid of frightening him. Oh no! On the contrary, I hinted that his nose might even collapse. I recounted what lay ahead for my patient in the event of his not receiving proper treatment. I touched upon the question of the infectiousness of syphilis, and talked for a long time about plates, spoons and cups and about a separate towel...

"Are you married?" I asked.

"I am," the patient responded in amazement.

"Send your wife to me at once!" I said with anxiety and passion. "She's probably sick as well, isn't she?"

"The wife?!" the patient enquired, and peered at me in great surprise.

And that was how we continued the conversation. Blinking, he looked into my pupils, and I into his. To be more accurate, it wasn't a conversation, but a monologue from me. A brilliant monologue, for which any professor would have given a top mark to a final-year student. I discovered that I had the most enormous knowledge in the sphere of syphilology, and exceptional gumption too. The latter filled the dark holes in the places where there were insufficient lines from German and Russian textbooks. I recounted what can happen to the bones of an untreated syphilitic, and at the same time outlined progressive paralysis too. His progeny! And how was his wife to be saved? Or, if she was infected, and she was *bound* to be infected, how was she to be treated?

Finally my flow dried up, and with a shy movement I took from my pocket a handbook in a red binding with gold lettering.

My faithful friend, with which I never parted during the first steps of my difficult journey. How many times did it come to my rescue, when accursed questions of prescription-writing opened up a black abyss before me! Stealthily, while the patient was getting dressed, I leafed through the pages and found what I needed.

Mercury ointment is a great remedy.

"You're going to give yourself rubs. You'll be given six sachets of ointment. You'll rub in one sachet a day... like this..."

And I demonstrated graphically and with ardour how the rubbing in should be done by rubbing my empty palm on my white coat...

"…Today rub it into your arm, tomorrow into your leg, then again into your arm – the other one. When you've given yourself six rubs, you'll wash yourself and come and see me. Without fail. Do you hear? Without fail! Yes! Apart from that, while you're being treated you need to keep a careful eye on your teeth and on your mouth in general. I'll give you a gargle. Be sure to rinse after food…"

"My throat too?" asked the patient hoarsely, and at this point I noticed that at the word "gargle" he had perked up.

"Yes, yes, your throat too."

A few minutes later the yellow back of his sheepskin coat was going out of sight through the doors, and squeezing in towards his back was a peasant woman's head in a scarf.

And a few minutes later still, while running down the half-dark corridor from my surgery to the pharmacy for cigarettes, I fleetingly heard a hoarse whisper:

"His treatment's no good. He's young. You see, my throat's blocked, and he looks and looks… first my chest, then my stomach. There's loads to do just now, and I've spent half a day in the hospital. By the time I get started out, it'll already be night. Oh Lord! I've got a sore throat, and he gives me ointments for my legs."

"No consideration, no consideration," confirmed a woman's voice with a certain jingle to it, but it suddenly stopped short. That was me, flashing by like a ghost in my white coat. I couldn't resist, I looked round and in the semi-darkness recognized the little beard, like a beard made of tow, and the swollen eyelids and the chicken's eye. And I recognized the voice with its menacing hoarseness too. I drew my head into my shoulders, shrank down in a furtive sort of way, as though I were at fault, and disappeared, distinctly feeling a certain injury burning in my soul. I was horrified.

Surely it hadn't all been for nothing?…

...It couldn't have been! And every morning for a month, at each surgery, I looked carefully through the surgery book like a detective, expecting to encounter the name of the wife of the attentive listener to my monologue on syphilis. For a month I expected him himself. But I didn't get to see anyone. And a month later he had expired in my memory, ceased to worry me, been forgotten...

Because more and more new people were coming, and every day of my work in the forgotten backwoods brought me astonishing incidents and tricky things, which made me wear my brain out, become flustered hundreds of times, then recover my presence of mind once more, and be inspired once more for the struggle.

Now, when many years have passed, far away from a forgotten, peeling white hospital, I remember the starry rash on his chest. Where is he? What is he doing? Oh, I know, I know. If he's alive, then he and his wife go to the local hospital from time to time. He complains of sores on his legs. I can clearly imagine the way he unwinds his foot bindings and looks for sympathy. And a young doctor, a man or a woman in a darned white coat, bends towards his legs, presses the bone above a lesion with a finger, looks for a reason. Finds it and writes in the book "Lues III".* Then asks whether he had ever been given a black ointment as treatment.

And then, just as I remember him, he will remember me, 1917, snow outside the window and six waxed paper sachets, six unused, sticky lumps.

"Yes, of course, of course I was..." he'll say, and he'll look with irony no longer, but with blackish alarm in his eyes. And the doctor will write him a prescription for potassium iodide, or perhaps prescribe another form of treatment. Will perhaps glance, just like me, at a handbook...

Greetings to you, my comrade!

...and, dearest wife, bow down low to Uncle Sofron Ivanovich for me. And besides that, dear wife, go and see our doctor, show yourself to him, as I've already been sick for six months with the venereal dizeaze of sifilis. But when I was home on leave, I didn't confide in you. Have treatment.

Your husband

An. Bukov.

The young woman stopped up her mouth with the end of her flannelette headscarf, sat down on the bench and began shaking with tears. Locks of her fair hair, wet with melted snow, had come out onto her forehead.

"Isn't he a swine? Eh?!" she cried out.

"He is a swine," I replied firmly.

Then came the most difficult and agonizing part. I had to calm her down. But how could I calm her down? To the hum of the voices of the people waiting impatiently in the waiting room, we spent a long time conversing in whispers...

Somewhere in the depths of my soul, yet to become blunted to human suffering, I sought out warm words. First of all I tried to kill the terror in her. Said that absolutely nothing was known yet, and she mustn't give way to despair ahead of the investigation. And there was no place for it after the investigation either: I told her about how successful we were in treating this venereal disease of syphilis.

"The swine, the swine," the young woman sobbed, choking on her tears.

"He is a swine," I echoed.

We spent quite a long time like this, giving abusive names to the "dearest husband" who had spent some time at home and then departed for the city of Moscow.

Finally the woman's face began to dry out, only the stains remained, and the eyelids over her black, despairing eyes were dreadfully swollen.

"What am I going to do? I've got two children, you know," she said in a dry, exhausted voice.

"Wait, wait," I mumbled, "we'll see what's to be done."

I called the midwife, Pelageya Ivanovna, and the three of us withdrew to a ward by itself where there was an obstetric chair.

"Oh, the wretch, oh, the wretch," Pelageya Ivanovna said huskily through her teeth. The woman was silent, her eyes were like two black holes, she peered through the window – into the dusk.

And this was one of the most thorough examinations in my life. Pelageya Ivanovna and I covered every inch of her body. And nowhere did I find anything suspicious.

"You know what," I said, and I felt a passionate desire for my hopes not to deceive me, and for no menacing, hard, primary lesion to appear anywhere later on, "you know what?… Stop worrying! There's hope. Hope. True, anything can still happen, but you've got nothing now."

"Nothing?!" the woman asked hoarsely. "Nothing?" Sparks appeared in her eyes, and a pink flush touched her cheekbones. "And what if it does come? Eh?…"

"I can't understand it myself," I said to Pelageya Ivanovna in a low voice, "judging by what she's said, she ought to be infected, and yet there's nothing."

"There's nothing," Pelageya Ivanovna responded like an echo.

We spoke in whispers with the woman for several minutes more about various time spans, about various intimate things, and I gave the woman instructions to keep coming to the hospital.

Now I looked at the woman and saw that she was a person

82

broken in two. Hope had crept into her, then straight away it had started to die. Once again she shed a few tears, and went away like a dark shadow. From that time on, a sword hung over the woman. Every Saturday she appeared soundlessly in my outpatients department. She grew very pinched, her cheekbones stood out more sharply, her eyes became sunken and surrounded by shadows. Concentrated thought pulled down the corners of her lips. With a customary gesture she would unwind her headscarf, then the three of us would go off to the ward. We would examine her.

The first three Saturdays passed, and still we found nothing on her. At that she began to recover a little. There was a lively glint appearing in her eyes, her face was reviving, the stretched mask was smoothing out. Our chances were growing. The danger was dwindling. On the fourth Saturday I already spoke with confidence. At my back was about ninety per cent in favour of a happy outcome. The renowned first twenty-one-day period had passed, and then some. There remained the remote chance of a lesion that is enormously late in developing. Finally those periods passed too, and one day, having felt her glands for the last time, I tossed the shining mirror aside into a basin and said to the woman:

"You're out of all danger. You needn't come back any more. This is a happy chance."

"And there won't be anything?" she asked in an unforgettable voice.

"Nothing."

I lack the skill to describe her face. I only remember her bowing low from the waist and disappearing.

She did, however, appear once more. In her hands was a package – two pounds of butter and two dozen eggs. And after a terrible battle I took neither the butter nor the eggs. And of this, because of my youth, I was very proud. But subsequently, when I was obliged to go hungry during the years of revolution, more than once I would remember the kerosene lamp, the black eyes and the golden lump of butter bearing her fingermarks, and with the dew standing out on it.

Why ever, when so many years have passed, have I now remembered her, doomed to four months of terror? Not without cause. That woman was my second patient in the sphere to which I subsequently gave my best years. The first was the one with the starry rash on his chest. And so she was the second patient, and the only exception: she was afraid. The only one in my memory, which has preserved the work done by the four of us (Pelageya Ivanovna, Anna Nikolayevna, Demyan Lukich and me) by the light of a kerosene lamp.

While her agonizing Saturdays went by in a sort of expectation of punishment, I started searching for "it". Autumn evenings are long. The tiled stoves in the doctor's apartment are hot. There was silence, and it seemed to me that I was alone in all the world with my lamp. Somewhere life was really raging, but outside my windows the slanting rain beat and tapped, then changed imperceptibly into soundless snow. For long hours I sat reading the old outpatients books for the preceding five years. Before me in their thousands and tens of thousands passed the names of people and the names of villages. In those columns of people I sought, and often found it. Inscriptions that were banal, dull, flashed by: "Bronchitis", "Laryngitis"... again and again... But there it is! "Lues III". Aha... And to one side, in sweeping writing, the customary hand has written:

Rp. Ung. hydrarg. ciner. 3.0 D.t.d...

There it is – the "black" ointment.

Once more. Once more bronchitises and catarrhs dance in my eyes and are suddenly interrupted... once again "Lues"...

Most of all there were notes specifically about secondary syphilis. Tertiary came up more rarely. And then it was potassium iodide that sweepingly occupied the "treatment" column.

The further I read the old outpatients folios, forgotten in the attic and smelling of mould, the more light was shed into my inexperienced head. I began to understand monstrous things.

Permit me, but where are the notes about a primary lesion? Not to be seen for some reason. In thousands and thousands of names there was, now and again, one, one. But endless lines of secondary syphilis. What ever does it mean? Well, this is what it means...

"It means..." I said in the shadows to myself, and to a mouse that was gnawing the old book spines on the bookshelves in the cupboard, "it means they have no idea about syphilis here, and that lesion doesn't frighten anyone. Yes, sir. And then it'll go and heal up. A scar will remain... Right, right, and nothing else? No, not nothing else! Secondary syphilis – and raging, too – will develop. When his throat is sore and damp papules appear on his body, Semyon Kotov, thirty-two, will come to the hospital and he'll be given the grey ointment... Aha!..."

A circle of light lay on the table, and the recumbent chocolate-coloured woman in the ashtray had disappeared under a heap of cigarette ends.

"I'm going to find this Semyon Kotov. Hm..."

The outpatients sheets, just touched by yellow decay, rustled. On 17th June 1916 Semyon Kotov received six sachets of the mercury healing ointment, invented long ago for Semyon Kotov's salvation. I know what my predecessor said to Semyon when handing him the ointment:

"Semyon, when you've rubbed all six in, you'll wash and come back here again. Do you hear, Semyon?"

Semyon, of course, bowed and said thank you in a husky voice. Let's see: ten or twelve days later, Semyon should appear in the book again without fail. Let's see, let's see... Smoke, the leaves rustle. Oh no, Semyon isn't here! Not ten days later, not twenty days later... He's not here at all. Ah, poor Semyon Kotov. So the marble rash must have disappeared, as the stars go out at dawn, the condylomata healed up. And he's going to die, Semyon is going to die for sure. I shall probably see this Semyon at my surgery with gummatous lesions. Is the skeleton of his nose intact? And does he have identical pupils?... Poor Semyon!

And here we have not Semyon, but Ivan Karpov. Nothing to wonder at. Why shouldn't Ivan Karpov fall ill? Yes, but permit me, why ever is he prescribed a small dose of calomel with lactose? Here's why: Ivan Karpov is two years old! But he has "Lues II"! The fateful number two! Ivan Karpov was brought here covered in stars, and lying in his mother's arms, he beat off the doctor's tenacious hands. I understand everything.

I know, I can guess, I realize where a little boy of two's primary lesion was, without which there can be nothing secondary. It was in his mouth! He got it from a spoon.

Teach me, backwoods! Teach me, silence of a house in the country! Yes, an old outpatients book can tell a young doctor many interesting things.

Above Ivan Karpov was: "Avdotya Karpova, 30."

Who's she? Ah, I understand. She's Ivan's mother. It was in her arms that he cried.

And below Ivan Karpov: "Maria Karpova, 8."

And who's she? His sister! Calomel...

There's a family here. A family. And there's only one person missing from it – Karpov, about thirty-five or forty... And I don't know what his name is – Sidor, Pyotr. Oh, that's unimportant!

"…dearest wife… the venereal dizeaze of sifilis…"

Here it is – the document. Light in my head. Yes, he probably arrived from the damned front and didn't "confide", or maybe didn't even know he needed to confide. He went away. And then it started. After Avdotya – Maria; after Maria – Ivan. A shared bowl of cabbage soup, a towel…

Here's another family. And another. There's an old man of seventy. "Lues II". An old man. What are you guilty of? Nothing. Of a shared mug. It's non-sexual, non-sexual. The light is clear. As clear and whitish as the early December dawn. So I had sat through the whole of my lonely night with the outpatients records and magnificent German textbooks with bright pictures.

Going off into my bedroom, I yawned and muttered:

"I'm going to fight 'it'."

To fight it you need to see it. And it didn't delay. The sleigh road opened, and I sometimes had a hundred people a day coming to see me. The day would break dull-white, and would end with black gloom outside the windows, into which gloom, mysteriously and with a quiet rustling, the last sledge would depart.

It passed before me varied and insidious. Now it would appear in the form of whitish lesions in a teenage girl's throat. Now in the form of legs bent like sabres. Now in the form of uneven, inert lesions on an old woman's yellow legs. Now in the form of wet papules on the body of a blossoming woman. Sometimes it occupied a forehead proudly in a half-moon crown of Venus. It appeared as a reflected punishment for the ignorance of their fathers on children with noses that looked like Cossack saddles. But apart from that, it slipped in without my noticing it too. Oh, I had come straight from the school desk, after all!

And I was working everything out for myself, and in solitude. It was hiding somewhere, both in bones and in minds.

I found out a lot of things.

"I was told to do the rubbing back then."

"With black ointment?"

"Black ointment, sir, black…"

"Crosswise? Today an arm, tomorrow a leg?"

"Yes, indeed. And how did you know that, good sir?" (Flatteringly.)

"How on earth could I fail to know?" I thought. "Oh, how could I fail. There it is – a gumma!…"

"Have you had venereal disease?"

"What do you mean! It's never been heard of in our family."

"Aha… Have you had a sore throat?"

"Throat? I have. Last year."

"Aha… And did Leonty Leontyevich give you an ointment?"

"Yes, indeed! As black as a boot."

"You made a poor job of rubbing in the ointment, Dad. A very poor job!…"

I squandered countless kilos of grey ointment. I prescribed lots and lots of potassium iodide and disgorged lots of passionate words. I succeeded in getting some people back after the first six rubs. With a few I succeeded, although for the most part not entirely, in giving the first courses of injections. But the majority slipped through my hands like sand in an hourglass, and I couldn't seek them out in the snowy gloom. Oh dear, I became convinced that the very reason syphilis was frightening here was that it wasn't frightening. That's why at the beginning of this reminiscence of mine I cited that woman with the black eyes. And I remembered her with a sort of warm respect precisely because of her fear. But she was alone!

* * *

I matured, I became single-minded, at times sullen. I dreamt of when my time would end and I would return to the university city, and there my battle would become easier.

On one such gloomy day, a woman came into my surgery in the outpatients department, young and very good-looking. In her arms she was carrying a child all muffled up, while two children tumbled in behind her, toddling and stumbling in felt boots of excessive size, as they held on to the blue skirt that stuck out from beneath her sheepskin jacket.

"A rash has fallen upon the children," the rosy-cheeked lassie said pompously.

I cautiously touched the forehead of the little girl who was holding on to her skirt. And she disappeared without trace into its folds. I fished the uncommonly fat-faced Vanka out of the skirt on the other side. Touched him too. And the forehead of neither was hot, they were both normal.

"Undress one of the children, my dear."

She undressed the little girl. The little naked body was dotted no less than the sky on a cold and frosty night. She had the blotches of a rosy rash and wet papules from head to foot. Vanka took it into his head to defend himself and howl. Demyan Lukich came and helped me…

"A cold, is it?" said the mother, looking on with serene eyes.

"O-oh, oh, a cold," grumbled Lukich, twisting his mouth in both compassion and disgust. "They've got colds like that all over the Korobovo district."

"And what's the cause of it?" asked the mother, while I examined her dappled sides and chest.

"Get dressed," I said.

Then I sat down at the desk, lay my head on my hand and yawned. (She was one of the last to come and see me that day, and her number was ninety-eight.) Then I spoke:

"You, lady, and your children too, have got 'the great pox'. A dangerous, terrible disease. You must all start having treatment at once, and continue having the treatment for a long time."

What a shame that it's hard to depict in words the mistrust in the woman's bulging blue eyes. She turned the baby round like a log in her arms, looked obtusely at its legs and asked:

"And where's it come from?"

Then she gave a crooked grin.

"Where from isn't of interest," I responded, lighting up my fiftieth cigarette of the day, "you'd do better to ask something else, what will become of your children if you don't have them treated."

"What, then? Nothing'll become of them," she replied, and began wrapping the baby up in its swaddling clothes.

My watch lay in front of me on the table. I remember, as if it were now, that I spoke for no more than three minutes before the woman broke into sobs. And I was very glad of those tears, because only thanks to them, provoked by my deliberately harsh and frightening words, did the subsequent part of the conversation become possible.

"And so, they're staying. Demyan Lukich, you'll put them in the wing. We'll manage with the typhus patients in ward two. Tomorrow I'll go into town and get permission to open an in-patients department for syphilitics."

Great interest blazed up in the *feldsher*'s eyes.

"What are you thinking of, Doctor?" he responded (he was a great sceptic). "How on earth are we going to manage on our own? What about the medicines? There are no spare nurses… And the preparation?… And the utensils, syringes?!"

But obtusely, obstinately, I shook my head and responded:

"I'll get them."

* * *

A month passed…

In three rooms of the little wing, buried in snow, there burned lamps with tin shades. On the beds the linen was torn. There were only two syringes. A little one-gram one and a five-gram Luer.* In short, there was pitiful poverty, buried in snow. But… Proudly apart lay the syringe, using which, and mentally freezing in terror, I had already several times given the infusions of salvarsan* that were new to me, and still mysterious and difficult.

And another thing: I felt much more tranquil at heart – there were seven men and five women in the wing, and with each day the starry rash was melting away before my very eyes.

It was evening. Demyan Lukich was holding a little lamp and casting light on shy Vanka. His mouth was smeared with semolina. But no longer were there any stars on him. And so all four passed under the lamp, comforting my conscience.

"So I'll be discharged tomorrow, then," said the mother, adjusting her blouse.

"No, it's not possible yet," I replied, "you'll have to undergo one more course."

"I don't consent," she replied, "there's loads to be done at home. Thank you for your help, but discharge us tomorrow. We're already well."

The conversation flared up like a bonfire. It ended like this:

"You… you know," I said, and sensed that I was turning crimson, "you know… you're a fool!…"

"What are you doing, using bad words? What sort of behaviour's that – using bad words?"

"And is it 'a fool' I should be calling you? No, not a fool, but… but!… Just take a look at Vanka! What, do you want to kill him? Well, I won't allow you to do it!"

And she stayed for another ten days.

Ten days! No one could have held her any longer. That I guarantee you. But, believe me, my conscience was tranquil, and even… "a fool" didn't trouble me. I don't repent. What's abuse in comparison with the starry rash!

And so time has gone by. Fate and tempestuous years parted me long ago from that wing buried in snow. What's there now, and who? I have faith that it's better. The building is whitewashed, perhaps, and the linen is new. Of course, there's no electricity. It may be that now, as I write these lines, someone's young head is bending towards a patient's chest. A kerosene lamp casts a yellowish light onto yellowish skin…

Greetings, my comrade!

The Missing Eye

A ND SO A YEAR has passed. It's exactly a year since I drove up to this very house. And just as now, there was a shroud of rain hanging outside the windows, and the last yellow leaves were drooping just as miserably on the birch trees. Nothing around would seem to have changed. But I myself have changed greatly. In complete solitude I shall celebrate an evening of memories...

And I walked over the creaking floor into the bedroom and looked in the mirror. Yes, the difference is huge. Reflected in the mirror taken out of the suitcase a year before there was a shaved face. A side parting then adorned my twenty-three-year-old head. Today the parting has disappeared. The hair is tossed back with no particular pretensions. You won't attract anyone with your parting thirty versts from the railway. And it's the same as regards shaving. Firmly established above the upper lip is a strip that resembles a rough, yellowed toothbrush, the cheeks have become like a grater, so that if my forearm starts itching while I'm working, it's pleasant to scratch it with my cheek. It's always the way if you shave not three times a week, but only once.

Now I read sometime, somewhere... where, I've forgotten... about an Englishman who landed up on an uninhabited island.* He was an interesting Englishman. He stayed on the island so long, he even had hallucinations. And when a ship approached the island, and a boat dispatched a rescue party, he – a recluse – greeted them with revolver fire, taking them for a mirage, a deception of the empty

93

expanse of water. But he was shaved. He shaved every day on an uninhabited island. I recall how that proud son of Britain aroused in me the most immense respect. And when I was coming here, there lay in my suitcase a Gillette safety razor with a dozen blades, and a cut-throat razor, and a brush. And I made a firm resolution to shave every other day, because where I was here was in no way inferior to an uninhabited island.

But then one day, it was in bright April, I laid out all those English delights in a slanting golden ray of sun, and had only just finished putting a gloss on my right cheek when in burst Yegorych, clattering like a horse in great ripped boots, and announced that a woman was in labour in some bushes by the reserve above the little river. I recall how I wiped my left cheek with a towel and swept out along with Yegorych. And three of us ran towards the river, turbid and swollen amidst bare clumps of willow bushes – a midwife with torsion forceps, a bundle of gauze and a jar of iodine, I with wild, goggling eyes, and Yegorych in the rear. Every five steps he would sit down on the ground, cursing, and tear at his left boot: its sole had come off. The wind was flying towards us, the sweet, wild wind of the Russian spring, the comb had slipped from Pelageya Ivanovna the midwife's head, her knot of hair was in disarray and was slapping against her shoulder.

"Why the devil do you squander all your money on drink?" I muttered to Yegorych on the wing. "It's swinish. Hospital watchman, but you go around like a tramp."

"You can't call it money," snapped Yegorych angrily, "you go through sheer torture for twenty roubles a month... Oh, damn you!" he beat the ground with his foot like a frenzied trotting horse. "Money... boots are neither here nor there when there's no money to buy food and drink with..."

"And it's the drink that's most important to you," I croaked, panting, "and that's why you loaf about like a ragamuffin…"

By a little rotten bridge we heard a faint mournful cry, it flew out above the swiftly flowing flood water and died away. We ran up and saw a dishevelled, contorted woman. Her headscarf had fallen off and her hair was stuck to her sweaty forehead, she was rolling her eyes in agony and ripping the sheepskin coat she wore with her fingernails. Bright blood stained the first, sparse, pale-green grass to have come out on the rich, waterlogged earth.

"She didn't reach us, she didn't reach us," said Pelageya Ivanovna hurriedly, bareheaded herself, and looking like a witch as she unwound her bundle.

And right there, listening to the cheerful roar of the water tearing between the darkened log piers of the bridge, Pelageya Ivanovna and I delivered a male baby. We delivered him alive, and we saved the mother. Then, with his left foot bare, freed at last from the hateful rotted sole, Yegorych and two nurses carried the woman over to the hospital on a stretcher.

When she lay, quiet now and pale, covered up with sheets, when the baby had been placed in a cradle beside her and everything put in order, I asked her:

"How did that happen, mother, couldn't you find a better place to give birth than on a bridge? Why didn't you come with a horse?"

She replied:

"My father-in-law wouldn't give me the horse. It's only five versts, he says, you'll get there. You're a healthy woman. There's no point in using the horse for nothing…"

"Your father-in-law's a fool and a swine," I responded.

"Oh, how ignorant the people are," Pelageya Ivanovna added pitifully, and then for some reason sniggered.

I caught her gaze; it was fixed on my left cheek.

I went out, and in the delivery room looked in the mirror. The mirror showed what it usually did: the twisted physiognomy of an obviously degenerate sort with what looked like a black right eye. But – and for this the mirror wasn't to blame – you could have danced on the degenerate's right cheek as if on a parquet floor, while on the left one there was a stretch of dense, reddish growth. The chin served as the dividing line. A book in a yellow binding with the inscription *Sakhalin** came to mind. There were photographs of various men in it.

"Murder, burglary, a bloodstained axe," I thought, "ten years... What an original life I do lead, after all, on this uninhabited island. I must go and finish shaving..."

Breathing in the April air, borne here from the black fields, I listened to the din of the crows coming from the tops of the birches, and squinted in the first sun as I went across the yard to finish shaving. It was about three o'clock in the afternoon. And I finished shaving at nine in the evening. Never, as far as I could see, did such unexpected things as labour in the bushes come singly at Muryevo. No sooner had I taken hold of the catch of the door on my porch than a horse's face appeared in the gateway, and a cart plastered with mud gave a violent lurch. A peasant woman was driving and crying in a thin voice:

"Gee up, you demon!"

And from the porch I heard a little boy in a heap of rags whimpering.

He turned out to have a broken leg, of course, and so for two hours the *feldsher* and I were busy putting a plaster cast on the little boy, who howled for two hours on end. Then I had to have dinner, and then I couldn't be bothered shaving, I fancied having a read of something, and then the dusk crept down, the distances closed in and, frowning mournfully, I did finish shaving. But since the cogged Gillette had been lying forgotten in soapy water, there was a little strip of rust left on it for ever as a memento of that springtime labour by the bridge.

No... there was no reason to shave twice a week. At times we were snowed in completely, an unimaginable blizzard would howl, we would sit for two days at a time in the Muryevo Hospital and didn't even send to Voznesensk, nine versts away, for newspapers; for long evenings I would keep on pacing out the length of my study and wishing avidly for some papers, as avidly as I had thirsted for Fenimore Cooper's *The Pathfinder** in childhood. But English quirks didn't die out entirely on the uninhabited island of Muryevo, and from time to time I would take my shiny toy out of its little black case and have a sluggish shave, coming out smooth and clean like a proud islander. It was just a shame that there was no one to admire me.

Permit me... yes... I mean, there was another incident too, when, as I recall, I had taken out the razor, and Aksinya had just brought a dented mug of boiling water into the study, when there was a menacing knock at the door and I was called out. And Pelageya Ivanovna and I drove a terribly long way, muffled up in sheepskin coats and rushing like a black spectre, comprised of the horses, the driver and us, through an enraged white ocean. The snowstorm hissed like a witch, it howled, spat and cackled, everything had gone to the devil and vanished, and I felt a familiar growing coldness somewhere in the region of my solar plexus at the thought that we would lose our way in this satanic swirling gloom and all disappear in the night: Pelageya Ivanovna, the driver, the horses and I. The foolish idea also came to me, I remember, that when we were freezing and half-covered in snow, I would inject the midwife, and the driver, and myself with morphine... Why? Simply so as not to suffer. "You'll make an excellent job of freezing, physician, without any morphine," a dry, sound voice answered me, I recall, "and it serves you right…" Oo-whoo-whoo!… Whoosh!… hissed the witch, and we were rocked and rocked about in the sledge… Well, on the back page of one of the capital's newspapers they'll say something to the effect that in the execution of their official duties, physician So-and-so, as well as Pelageya Ivanovna and the driver and a pair of horses, perished. May they rest in peace in the snowy sea. Pah… the things that come into your head when you're being borne on and on by so-called official duty…

We neither died, nor got lost, but arrived in the village of Grischevo, where I began performing the second podalic version of my life. The woman in labour was the wife of the village teacher, and while Pelageya Ivanovna and I were struggling with the version by the light of a lamp, with blood up to our elbows and sweat in our eyes, the husband could be heard outside the plank door, groaning and wandering around beyond the hut's living quarters. To the woman's groans and his incessant sobbing, I'll tell you in confidence, I broke the baby's arm. The baby was dead when we delivered him. Oh, how the sweat ran down my back! It instantly came into my head that someone menacing, black and huge would come bursting into the hut and in a stony voice say: "Aha. Take his degree away!"

Exhausted, I gazed at the little, yellow dead body and the waxen mother who lay motionless, rendered oblivious by chloroform. A blast of the blizzard was beating at the transom window, which we opened for a minute to rarefy the stifling smell of the chloroform, and the blast turned into a cloud of steam. Then I slammed the transom shut and once more fastened my gaze on the helplessly dangling little arm in the arms of the midwife. Oh, I can't express the despair in which I returned home alone, because I left Pelageya Ivanovna to care for the mother. I was tossed about in the sledge in the abating snowstorm, gloomy forests looked on reproachfully, hopelessly, desperately. I felt myself defeated, broken, crushed by cruel Fate. It had tossed me into these backwoods and forced me to struggle alone, without any support or instructions. What unbelievable difficulties I was obliged to endure. I might be brought any tricky or complex case whatsoever, more often than not surgical, and I had to face up to it with my unshaven face and defeat it. And if you didn't defeat it, then suffer torment, as now, when you were dragged over a bumpy road, while the little corpse of a baby remained behind with its mummy. The next day, as soon as the blizzard died down, Pelageya Ivanovna would bring her to me at the hospital, and there was one very big question – would I be able to preserve her? Yes, and how was I to *preserve* her? How was that grand word to be understood? In essence, I acted haphazardly, I didn't know anything. Well, up until now I'd been lucky, I'd got away with some amazing things, but today I'd been out of luck. Oh, my heart ached from loneliness, from the cold, from having no one around. And perhaps I had committed a crime too – the arm. I ought to go somewhere, fall at someone's feet and say something to the effect that: "I, physician So-and-so, have broken a baby's arm. Take my degree away, I'm unworthy of it, dear colleagues, send me to Sakhalin." Ugh, neurasthenia!

I collapsed onto the bottom of the sledge, huddling myself up so that the cold didn't bite into me so terribly, and I seemed to myself like a pitiful little dog, a mutt, homeless and clumsy.

We drove for a long, long time before the lamp by the gates of the hospital flashed out, small, but so joyous, eternally dear. It twinkled, melted away, flared up and disappeared again, drawing you towards it. And my lonely soul was somewhat eased on looking at the lamp, and when it was already firmly established before my eyes, when it was growing and approaching, when the walls of the hospital were turning from black to whitish, as I rode in through the gates, this is what I was already saying to myself:

"The arm's nonsense. It has no significance. You broke it when the baby was already dead. You need to think not about the arm, but about the fact that the mother's alive."

The lamp cheered me up, the familiar porch too, but all the same, when I was already inside the house, going up to my study, feeling the warmth from the stove and looking forward to sleep, that deliverer from all torment, this is what I muttered:

"That's all well and good, but nevertheless, I'm frightened and lonely. Very lonely."

The razor lay on the table, and beside it stood the mug of boiling water, now cold. I tossed the razor into a drawer with contempt. I really, really must have a shave...

And now it's been a whole year. While it was dragging on, it seemed many-sided, diverse, complex and strange, though now I can see that it flew by like a hurricane. But as I look in the mirror, I can see the mark it has left on my face. My eyes have become sterner and more anxious, while my mouth is more confident and manly, the crease on the bridge of my nose will remain for the rest of my life, as will my memories. I can see them in the mirror, they run by in a turbulent sequence. When, if you please, I still shook at the thought of my degree, of some fantastic court trying me and dread judges asking:

"And where is the soldier's jaw? Answer, you villain of a university graduate!"

How can I fail to remember! The thing was that, although there might be Demyan Lukich the *feldsher*, who pulls teeth just as adroitly as a carpenter pulls rusty nails from old planks, nonetheless, tact and self-respect told me during my very first steps at the Muryevo Hospital that I needed to learn to pull teeth myself as well. Demyan Lukich might be away or fall ill, and our midwives can do anything except for just the one: sorry, they don't pull teeth, that's not their job.

Therefore... I remember very well a physiognomy before me on the stool, ruddy, but wretched with suffering. He was a soldier who had returned along with others from the front, which had disintegrated after the Revolution. I have an excellent memory too of the most enormous, strong tooth sitting firmly with its cavity in his jaw. Narrowing my eyes with a wise expression and giving the occasional preoccupied quack, I fixed my pliers on the tooth, at the same time recalling distinctly, however, the Chekhov story that everyone knows about a sexton having a tooth pulled.* And it seemed to me then for the very first time that that story wasn't the least bit funny. There was a loud crunch in the soldier's mouth, and he gave a short howl:

"Oho-o!"

After that, the resistance beneath my hand ceased, and the pliers leapt out of his mouth with a bloodied and white object clamped in them. At that point my heart missed a beat, because this object exceeded the size of any tooth, even the soldier's molar. At first I couldn't understand a thing, but then I almost broke into sobs: poking out from the pliers there was, it's true, a tooth with extremely long roots, but hanging from the tooth was a huge piece of bright white, rough bone.

"I've broken his jaw..." I thought, and my legs buckled. Thanking Fate for the fact that neither the *feldsher*, nor the midwives were there beside me, with a furtive movement I wrapped up the fruit of my energetic work in gauze and put it in my pocket. The soldier was rocking on the stool with one hand gripping a leg of the obstetric chair and the other a leg of the stool, and he was looking at me with goggling, completely crazed eyes. Dismayed, I jabbed a glass with a solution of potassium permanganate at him:

"Rinse."

It was a stupid thing to do. He took a mouthful of the solution, and when he let it out into a cup, the solution ran out, mixed with the soldier's scarlet blood, turning on the way into a thick liquid of an unprecedented colour. After that, blood gushed out of the soldier's mouth in a way that made me freeze. Had I slashed the poor man's throat with a razor, it would scarcely have flowed more freely. Setting the glass of potassium aside, I fell upon the soldier with balls of gauze and stuffed up the gaping hole in his jaw. The gauze instantly became scarlet and, taking it out, I saw with horror that a good-sized greengage could easily be fitted into the hole.

"I've bashed the soldier up a real treat," I thought desperately, dragging long strips of gauze from a jar. Finally the blood died away, and I smeared iodine on the pit in his jaw.

"Don't eat anything for three hours or so," I said to my patient in a tremulous voice.

"I'm most humbly grateful to you," the soldier responded, gazing with a certain amazement into the cup that was full of his blood.

"You know what, my friend," I said in a pathetic voice, "you… you drop in tomorrow or the day after and let me see you. I'll… you see… I'll need to take a look… You've got another suspect tooth next door… All right?"

"We're most humbly grateful," the soldier replied sullenly, and he withdrew, holding on to his cheek, while I rushed into the surgery and sat there for some time, clutching my head in my hands and rocking as though I had toothache myself. Half a dozen times I pulled the hard, bloodstained lump out of my pocket, then hid it again.

For a week I lived as in a fog, became wasted and grew ill.

"The soldier's going to get gangrene, blood poisoning... Oh, damn it! Why did I use the pliers on him?"

Absurd pictures presented themselves to me. Here's the soldier starting to suffer from the shakes. At first he goes around talking of Kerensky* and the front, then becomes ever quieter. He doesn't care about Kerensky any longer. The soldier is lying on a cotton pillow, raving. His temperature is forty degrees. The whole village visits the soldier. And then the soldier is lying with a sharpened nose on a table beneath some icons.

Gossip starts up in the village.

"What could have caused it?"

"The dogter pulled one of his teeth out."

"So that's it..."

Then from bad to worse. An investigation. A stern man arrives.

"Was it you that pulled the soldier's tooth?..."

"Yes... me."

The soldier is exhumed. Trial. Disgrace. I am the cause of death. And now I'm no longer a doctor, but a wretched man thrown overboard, or, to be more accurate, a former man.

The soldier didn't appear, I was miserable and the lump went rust-coloured and dried out in my desk. The staff needed to go to the local town for their salaries a week later. I set off after five days, and went first of all to the doctor at the town's district hospital. With his little beard that smelt of tobacco smoke, this man had been working at the hospital for twenty-five years. He had seen a lot in his time. I sat in his study in the evening, drank lemon tea despondently, picking at the tablecloth, and was finally unable to bear it. Beating about the bush, I came out with a vague, artificial speech to the effect: "Are there ever such instances... if someone pulls a tooth... and breaks off some of the jaw...

I mean, you might get gangrene, mightn't you?... You know, a piece... I've read..."

He listened and listened, fixing me with his faded little eyes beneath shaggy brows, and this is what he suddenly said:

"It was you that broke off his tooth socket... You'll be great at pulling teeth... Leave the tea, we'll go and have some vodka before dinner."

And the soldier who had been tormenting me went out of my head at once, and for ever.

Ah, the mirror of memories. A year has passed. How funny I find it, remembering that tooth socket! True, I shall never pull teeth like Demyan Lukich. No wonder! He pulls half a dozen every day, while once in two weeks I pull one. But all the same, I pull them as many would like to. And I don't break tooth sockets, and even if I did, I wouldn't take fright.

But teeth aren't the half of it. What haven't I seen and what haven't I done in the course of this unrepeatable year!

The evening was flowing into the room. The lamp was already lit and, floating in bitter tobacco smoke, I was summing things up. My heart was overflowing with pride. I had performed two amputations at the hip, and I wasn't counting the number of fingers and toes. And the irrigations. I have them noted down eighteen times. And a hernia. And a tracheotomy. I've done one, and it turned out successfully. How many gigantic abscesses had I lanced! And bandages for fractures. Plaster and starch ones. I've set dislocations. Intubations. Childbirth – come with any kind you like. I wouldn't think of performing a Caesarean section, it's true. That can be sent to town. But forceps, versions – as many as you like.

I remember the final public examination on forensic medicine. The professor said:

"Tell me about wounds at point-blank range."

I began telling him in a relaxed way, and continued for a long time, as a page from an extremely thick textbook swam by in my visual memory. Finally I was played out, the professor looked at me fastidiously and said in a rasping voice:

"Nothing like what you have been saying is ever found in wounds at point-blank range. How many fives do you have?"

"Fifteen," I replied.

He put a three against my name,* and I left the room in a haze and in shame...

I left the room, and then soon came to Muryevo, and now here I am alone. The devil knows what *is* found in wounds at point-blank range, but when a man lay here before me on the operating table, and bubbly froth, pink with blood, was bursting up on his lips, did I lose my composure? No, although the whole of his chest had been sprayed with buckshot at point-blank range, and a lung was visible, and the meat on his chest hung in shreds, did I lose my composure? And a month and a half later I had him leave the hospital alive. Not once at university did I have the honour of holding obstetric forceps in my hands, while here, trembling it's true, I had applied them in a minute. I can't conceal the fact that I delivered a strange baby: half of its head was swollen, bluish-purple, eyeless. I went cold. Vaguely heard out Pelageya Ivanovna's words of comfort:

"Never mind, Doctor, you put one of the spoons on its eye."

I was shaking for two days, but after two days the head had returned to normal.

What wounds I'd sewn up. What cases of purulent pleurisy had I seen, and what ribs hadn't I broken in connection with them, what cases of pneumonia, typhus, cancer, syphilis, what hernias (which I'd set), haemorrhoids, sarcomas.

Inspired, I opened up the outpatients book and spent an hour counting. And counted everything up. Over the year, up to that evening hour, I had seen 15,613 patients. I had had two hundred in-patients, and only six had died.

I shut the book and trudged off to sleep. A twenty-four-year-old celebrating an anniversary, I lay in bed and, as I was falling asleep, thought about the fact that my experience was now enormous. What was there for me to fear? Nothing. I had pulled peas out of little boys' ears, I had cut, cut, cut... My hand is manly and doesn't tremble. I had seen all sorts of tricks and learnt to understand the kinds of women's talk that no one else would. I knew them in the way Sherlock Holmes knew mysterious documents... Sleep was ever closer...

"I simply can't imagine," I muttered, as I was falling asleep, "being brought a case that would have me nonplussed... maybe there, in the capital, they'd say that this was feldsherism... let them... it's all right for them... in clinics, in universities... in X-ray rooms... but I'm here... and that's it... and the peasants can't live without me... How I used to tremble at a knock on the door, how I used to cringe mentally with fear... But now..."

"When ever did this happen?"

"About a week ago, sir, about a week, my dear... It popped out..."

And the peasant woman started whimpering.

Looking on was the rather grey October morning of the first day of my second year. The evening before I had been feeling proud and boasting as I fell asleep, but this morning I stood in my white coat and peered in perplexity...

She was holding a one-year-old boy in her arms like a log, and this little boy had no left eye. In place of the eye, poking out from the stretched, attenuated lids was a yellow-coloured ball the size of a small apple. The little boy was crying out in suffering and struggling, and the woman was whimpering. And here I lost my composure.

I went at it from every angle. Demyan Lukich and a mid-wife stood behind me. They were silent, they had never seen anything like it.

"What is it?..." I thought. "A rupture of the brain... Hm... he's alive... A sarcoma... Hm... it's quite soft... Some sort of unprecedented, terrible tumour... Where on earth has it developed from... From what used to be the eye... Or perhaps it was never actually there... In any event, it isn't there now..."

"Look here," I said, inspired, "I'm going to have to cut this thing out..."

And at once I pictured the way I would make an incision in the eyelid, pull it apart, and...

"And what?..." I thought. "And what next? Maybe it actually has come from the brain... Pah, damn it... It's quite soft... like the brain..."

"Cut what?" asked the woman, turning pale. "Cut his eye? You don't have my consent..."

And horrified, she began wrapping the baby up in bits of cloth.

"He hasn't got an eye," I replied categorically, "just look, where's it supposed to be? Your baby has a strange tumour..."

"Give us some drops," the woman said in horror.

"What, joking are you? What drops? There's no drops that will help here."

"What, then, he's to be left without an eye, is he?"

"He doesn't have an eye, I'm telling you."

"Well he did two days ago!" the woman exclaimed despairingly.

"Damn!..." I thought.

"I don't know, perhaps he did... damn... but now he doesn't... All in all, you know what, my dear, take your baby into town. And at once, they'll operate on him there. Demyan Lukich. Eh?"

"Y-yes," the *feldsher* responded profoundly, obviously not knowing what to say, "the thing's unprecedented."

"Do the cutting in town?" the woman asked in horror. "I won't allow it."

In the end the woman took her baby away without allowing its eye to be touched.

For two days I racked my brains, shrugged my shoulders, rummaged in my library, looked out for drawings in which babies were depicted with things ballooning out of them in place of eyes... Damn.

But after two days I forgot about the baby.

A week passed.

"Anna Zhukhova!" I called.

In came a cheerful peasant woman with a child in her arms.

"What's the matter?" I asked in my customary way.

"My sides are aching, I can't breathe properly," the woman informed me, and for some reason gave me a mocking smile.

The sound of her voice gave me a start.

"Have you recognized me?" asked the woman mockingly.

"Hang on... hang on... what's this... Hang on... is this the same child?"

"The same one. Remember, Mr Doctor, you said the eye wasn't there and there had to be cutting..."

I was stupefied. The woman looked at me triumphantly, and there was laughter playing in her eyes.

The baby sat silently in her arms and gazed at me with its brown eyes. There was no trace of any yellow blister.

"This is some kind of sorcery..." I thought weakly.

Then, coming to my senses somewhat, I cautiously pulled the eyelid forward. The baby whimpered and tried to twist its head around, but I saw nonetheless... a tiny little scar on the mucous membrane... Aha...

"As soon as we left you t'other day... It went and burst..."

"There's no need, woman, don't tell me," I said, abashed, "I've already got it..."

"And you say there's no eye there... Look how one's grown." And the woman tittered impudently.

"Got it, the devil take me... the most enormous abscess developed from his lower eyelid, it grew and pushed back the eye, covering it up completely... and then when it burst, the pus flowed out... and everything fell back into place..."

No. Never, not even when falling asleep, will I ever proudly mutter about nothing being able to surprise me. No. As one year has passed, so will another, and it will be just as rich in surprises as the first one... And so I have to go on dutifully learning.

Morphine

I

C LEVER PEOPLE HAVE BEEN pointing out for a long time that happiness is like good health: when it's there, you don't notice it. But when the years have passed, how you do remember happiness, oh, how you do remember it!

As far as I'm concerned, I, as has now become apparent, was happy in 1917,* in the winter. An unforgettable, head-long year of blizzards!

The incipient blizzard caught me up like a scrap of torn newspaper and carried me from my remote district to a small provincial town. What's so special, you might think, about a small provincial town? But if someone has sat, like me, in snow in the winter, and in stern, sorry woods in the summer, for a year and a half, without being away for a single day, if someone has ripped open the postal wrapping on the previous week's newspaper with beating heart, the way a happy lover does a light-blue envelope, if someone has travelled eighteen versts to a woman in labour in a sledge with horses harnessed in single file, he, one must assume, will understand me.

A kerosene lamp is a very cosy thing, but I'm in favour of electricity!

And now I saw them again, at last, seductive electric lamps! The little town's main street, well smoothed down by peasants' sledges, the street in which, enchanting one's gaze, there hung a shop sign with boots on it, a golden pretzel, red flags and an image of a young man with insolent little piggy eyes and an utterly unnatural hairstyle, signifying that housed behind the glass doors was the local Basile,* who for thirty kopeks would undertake to shave you at any time, with the exception of the public holidays in which my fatherland abounds.

To this day I recall with a tremor the Basile's napkins, napkins which persistently made me imagine the page in a German textbook on skin diseases, on which was depicted, with convincing clarity, a hard chancre on some citizen's chin.

But all the same, even those napkins cannot cloud my memories!

At the crossroads stood a live policeman; dimly visible in a dusty shop window were iron trays, bearing crowded rows of fancy cakes with ginger-coloured buttercream; hay covered the square; people walked, and rode, and conversed; on sale in a booth were the previous day's Moscow papers containing stunning news; nearby, the Moscow trains exchanged whistles of invitation. In a word, this was civilization, Babylon, Nevsky Avenue.

And that's to say nothing of the hospital. It had a surgical department, therapeutic, infectious diseases, obstetric departments. There was an operating room at the hospital, and in it was a gleaming autoclave, there was the silver of taps, the tables revealed their intricate clamps, cogs, screws. There was a senior doctor at the hospital, three house surgeons (apart from me), *feldshers*, midwives, nurses, a pharmacy and a laboratory. A laboratory, just think of it! With a Zeiss microscope and a fine supply of dyes.

I would shudder and turn cold, I was crushed by my impressions. Not a few days passed before I got used to the fact that the single-storey buildings of the hospital would blaze out in the December dusk, as if by command, with electric light.

It dazzled me. Water raged and thundered in the baths, and begrimed wooden thermometers dived and floated about in them. All day in the children's-infectious-diseases department there were groans bursting out, there was thin, pitiful crying and hoarse gurgling to be heard...

Nurses ran about, hurried around...

A heavy burden slipped from my soul. No longer did I bear a fateful responsibility for anything that might happen in the world. I wasn't to blame for a strangulated hernia, and I didn't shudder when a sledge arrived bringing a woman with a transverse lie, I wasn't concerned with cases of purulent pleurisy requiring operations... For the first time I felt like a human being, whose degree of responsibility was limited by some sort of framework. Childbirth? If you please, over there there's a rather low building, and over there is the last window, curtained with white gauze. The obstetrician is there, likeable and fat, with a little ginger moustache and rather bald. That's his business. Sledge, turn towards the window with the gauze! A compound fracture – that's the chief surgeon. Pneumonia? To Pavel Vladimirovich in the therapeutic department.

Oh, the majestic machine of a large hospital in regulated, precisely oiled motion! Like a new screw made to measure in advance, I too entered into the machinery and took on the children's department. Both diphtheria and scarlatina absorbed me and took up my days. But only the days. I began sleeping at night, because no longer was the ominous nocturnal knocking to be heard beneath my windows, the knocking which might get me up and carry me away into the darkness to danger and the inexorable. In the evenings I started reading (about diphtheria and scarlatina in the first place, of course, and then, for some reason with strange interest, Fenimore Cooper) and was fully appreciative of the lamp over the desk, and of the grey coals on the tray with the samovar, and of the tea that grew cold, and of sleep after a sleepless year and a half...

Thus I was happy in the winter of 1917, having been transferred from a remote district of blizzards to a small provincial town.

II

A MONTH FLEW BY, AND after it a second and a third, 1917 receded, and February 1918 flew off. I had grown accustomed to my new position, and little by little began to forget my distant district. The green lamp with the hissing kerosene, the loneliness, the snowdrifts faded from my memory... Ingrate! I forgot my battle post where, alone, without any support, I had struggled with illnesses unaided, getting out of the most bizarre situations like a Fenimore Cooper hero.

Occasionally, it's true, when I was going to bed with the pleasant thought of how in a moment I would fall asleep, certain scraps would fly by in my already darkening consciousness. A little green light, a twinkling lamp... the squeaking of a sledge... a short groan, then darkness, the muffled howling of the snowstorm in the fields... Then it would all tumble aside and vanish...

"I wonder who's sitting there now in my place?... There must be someone... A young doctor like me... well, I sat my time out. February, March, April... well, and let's say May – and that's the end of my probation period. And so at the end of May I shall part with my brilliant town and return to Moscow. And if the Revolution catches me up on its wing – I may have to travel some more... but in any event I shall never in my life see my rural district again... Never... The capital... A clinic... Asphalt, lights..."

That's what I thought.

"But all the same, it's a good thing that I spent the time in that district... I became a courageous person... I'm not afraid... What didn't I treat?! Yes, really? Eh?... I didn't treat any mental illness... I mean... actually no, I'm sorry... The agronomist drank himself to the devil that time... And I treated him, rather unsuccessfully too... Delirium tremens... How does that differ from a mental illness? I ought to read some psychiatry... Oh, to hell with it... Sometime later on, in Moscow... But now, first and foremost, it's paediatrics... and more paediatrics... and in particular the drudgery that is prescription-writing for children... Ugh, damn it... If a child's ten, then how much, let's say, pyramidon* can it be given at a time? 0.1 or 0.15?... I've forgotten. And if the child's three?... Just paediatrics... and nothing more... enough of those mind-boggling surprises! Farewell, my rural district!... But why is the district coming to mind so insistently this evening?... The green light... I've settled my accounts with it for the rest of my life, haven't I... Enough now... Sleep..."

"There's a letter. It was brought by someone passing."

"Give it here."

The nurse was standing in my entrance hall. An overcoat with a threadbare collar had been thrown on over her white coat with its stamp on it. Snow was melting on the cheap blue envelope.

"Are you on duty in admissions today?" I asked with a yawn.

"I am."

"Is there no one there?"

"No, it's empty."

"Yif..." – a fit of yawning was tearing my mouth apart and making me pronounce words in a slovenly way – "anyone's brough' in... you jush let me know... I'm going to bed..."

"Very well. Can I go?"

"Yes, yes. You go."

She left. The door squealed, and I shuffled off in my slippers to the bedroom, my fingers tearing the envelope in a hideous, crooked way as I went.

Inside it was a crumpled, oblong prescription form bearing the blue stamp of my district, my hospital... An unforgettable form...

I grinned.

"That's interesting... I was thinking about the district all evening, and now it's turned up of its own accord to remind me of itself... A presentiment..."

Inscribed beneath the stamp in indelible pencil was a prescription. Latin words, illegible, crossed out...

"I don't understand a thing... A muddled prescription..." I muttered, and stared at the word "*morphini...*" "Now what's the extraordinary thing about this prescription here?... Ah, yes... A four-per cent solution! Who on earth prescribes a four-per cent solution of morphine?... What for?!"

I turned the sheet of paper over and my yawning fit passed. Written in ink on the reverse of the sheet in a limp and well-spaced hand, was:

11th February 1918.

Dear collega!
Forgive me for writing on this scrap. There's no paper to hand. I've fallen very gravely and badly ill. There's no one to help me, and I don't actually want to seek help from anyone but you.

For more than a month I've been working in your former district; I know you're in town and comparatively near me.

In the name of our friendship and university years, I'm asking you to come to me quickly. If only for a day. If only for an hour. And if you tell me mine is a hopeless case, I'll believe you... But perhaps I can be saved?... Yes, perhaps

119

I can still be saved?... Will there be a ray of hope for me?
Please, don't inform anyone of the content of this letter.

"Maria! Go to admissions straight away and send the duty nurse to me... What's her name?... Oh, I've forgotten... In short, the woman on duty who just brought me a letter. Quickly!"

"At once."

A few minutes later the nurse was standing in front of me, and snow was melting on the threadbare cat that served as the material for her collar.

"Who brought the letter?"

"I don't know. He had a beard. He's from the cooperative. He was going to town, he said."

"Hm... well, off you go. No, hang on. I'll just write a note to the head doctor; please take it, and bring me back the reply."

"Very well."

My note to the head doctor:

13th February 1918.

Respected Pavel Illarionovich. I've just received a letter from my university comrade Dr Polyakov. He's working in complete solitude at Gorelovo, my former district. He's fallen ill, evidently seriously. I consider it my duty to go to him. If you'll permit me, tomorrow I'll hand the department over for one day to Dr Rodovich and go and see Polyakov. The man is helpless.
Respectfully yours,
Dr Bomgard.

The head doctor's note in reply:

Respected Vladimir Mikhailovich, do go.

Petrov.

I spent the evening studying a guide to the railways. Gorelovo could be reached thus: by leaving next day at two o'clock in the afternoon on the Moscow post train, travelling thirty versts on the railway, getting off at the station of N***, and from there going twenty-two versts by sledge to the Gorelovo Hospital.

"With luck I'll be at Gorelovo tomorrow night," I thought, lying in bed. "What's he got? Typhus, pneumonia? Neither of them... Had that been the case he would have written simply: "I've got pneumonia." But here you have a confused, somewhat insincere letter... "Gravely... and badly ill..." What with? Syphilis? Yes, it's syphilis, without a doubt. He's horrified... he's concealing it... he's afraid... But what horses, I'd like to know, am I to use to travel to Gorelovo from the station? That'll be good, when I arrive at the station in the dusk, and there's no transport for me to use to reach him... But no. I'll find a way. I'll find someone with horses at the station. Or send a telegram for him to send out horses! No point! The telegram will arrive a day after I get there... It won't fly through the air to Gorelovo, after all. It'll be lying at the station until there's someone to take it. I know that Gorelovo. Oh, it's a godforsaken spot!"

The letter on the form lay on my night table in the circle of light from the lamp, and next to it was the companion of my irritable insomnia with its stubble of cigarette butts, the ashtray. I tossed and turned on my crumpled sheet, and vexation sprang up in my soul. The letter began to irritate me.

"After all, if it's nothing acute, but, let's say, syphilis, then why ever doesn't he come here himself? Why should I race through a blizzard to him? What, will I cure him of lues in one evening, or something? Or of cancer of the oesophagus? What am I talking about, cancer! He's two years younger than me. He's twenty-five... "Gravely..." A sarcoma? It's a ridiculous, hysterical letter. A letter that might give the recipient a migraine... And there it is. Tightening the vein on my temple... So you'll wake in the morning, and it'll go up from the vein to your crown, it'll fetter half your head, and by evening you'll be swallowing pyramidon and caffeine. And what are you going to be like in the sledge with pyramidon?! You'll have to get a travelling fur coat from the *feldsher*, you'll freeze in your overcoat tomorrow... What's the matter with him? "Will there be a ray of hope..." – people write like that in novels, but certainly not in serious doctors' letters!... Sleep, sleep... Don't think about it any more. Everything will become clear tomorrow... Tomorrow."

I turned the switch off, and the darkness devoured my room instantly. Sleep... The vein is aching... But I have no right to get angry with a man over a ridiculous letter when I don't yet know what's wrong. A man is suffering in his own particular way, and here he is writing to another. Well, in the way he knows, the way he understands... And it's unworthy to denigrate him, even in my mind, because of a migraine, because of anxiety. Maybe it's neither an insincere, nor a novelish letter. I haven't seen him for two years, Seryozha Polyakov, but I remember him very well. He was always a very sensible man... Yes. That means some kind of misfortune has befallen him... And my vein feels better... Sleep's evidently on its way. What's the mechanism of sleep?... I read about it in a book on physiology... but it's an obscure business... I don't understand what sleep means... how do the brain cells fall asleep?! I'll tell you in confidence, I don't understand it. And for some reason I'm sure that even the compiler of that book on physiology himself isn't very definitely sure either... One theory's as good as another... There's Seryozha Polyakov standing over a zinc table in a green double-breasted jacket with gold buttons, and on the table is a corpse...

Hm, yes... now that's a dream...

III

KNOCK, KNOCK... BANG, BANG, bang... Aha... Who is it? Who is it? What is it?... Oh, someone's knocking, oh, damn, someone's knocking... Where am I? What am I doing?... What's the matter? Yes, in my own bed... Why on earth are they waking me up? They have every right, because I'm on duty. Wake up, Dr Bomgard. There goes Maria, shuffling to the door to open up. What's the time? Half-past twelve... It's night-time. So I was asleep for only an hour. How's the migraine? It's there. There it is!

There was a quiet knock at the door.

"What's the matter?"

I opened the door into the dining room just a little. The nurse's face looked at me from the darkness, and I made out at once that it was pale, that the eyes were widened, agitated.

"Who's been brought in?"

"The doctor from the Gorelovo district," the nurse replied in a loud, hoarse voice. "The doctor's shot himself."

"Pol-ya-kov? That's not possible! Polyakov?!"

"I don't know his name."

"Listen... I'm on my way now, right now. And you run to the head doctor, wake him up this second. Tell him I'm summoning him urgently to admissions."

The nurse rushed off – and the white blot vanished from my eyes.

Two minutes later the angry blizzard, dry and prickly, lashed my cheeks on the porch, blew out the skirts of my overcoat and turned my frightened body to ice.

In the windows of the admissions ward blazed a white, restless light. On the porch, in a cloud of snow, I ran into the senior doctor who was speeding to the same place as me.

"Your man? Polyakov?" asked the surgeon, coughing a little.

"I can't understand a thing. It's evidently him," I replied, and we speedily went into admissions.

A woman, all wrapped up, rose from a bench to meet us. Familiar, tearstained eyes looked at me from under the bottom of a brown headscarf. I recognized Maria Vlasyevna, a midwife from Gorelovo, my faithful assistant during childbirth at the Gorelovo Hospital.

"Polyakov?" I asked.

"Yes," replied Maria Vlasyevna, "it was awful, Doctor, I was trembling all the way as I was driving, I just had to get him here…"

"When?"

"This morning at dawn," muttered Maria Vlasyevna, "a watchman came running and says… 'There's been a shot in the doctor's apartment…'"

Under a lamp, which shed a horrid, alarming light, lay Dr Polyakov, and from my very first glance at the soles of his felt boots, lifeless, as though made of stone, my heart missed a beat in its customary way.

His hat was removed, revealing damp hair, all stuck together. Hands began flashing over Polyakov, my hands, the nurse's and Maria Vlasyevna's, and white gauze with spreading yellow and red patches emerged from under his overcoat. His chest was rising weakly. I felt his pulse and faltered, the pulse kept disappearing under my fingers, stretching out and breaking into a thread with little knots, frequent and fragile. The surgeon's hand was already stretching out towards his shoulder, pinching the pale body at the shoulder in order to inject camphor. And here the wounded man parted his lips, at which a pinkish bloody stripe appeared on them, and stirring his blue lips a little, in a dry, weak voice he said:

"Don't bother with camphor. To hell with it."

"Be quiet," the surgeon answered him and squeezed the yellow oil in under the skin.

"One has to assume that the pericardial sac's been affected," whispered Maria Vlasyevna, taking a firm grip on the edge of the table and starting to peer at the wounded man's unending eyelids (his eyes were closed). Violet-grey shadows, like the shadows of sunset, began to blossom ever more vividly in the depressions by the wings of his nose, and little beads of sweat, as if of mercury, were standing out like dew on the shadows.

"A revolver?" asked the surgeon, with a twitch of his cheek.

"A Browning," babbled Maria Vlasyevna.

"O-oh dear," the surgeon said all of a sudden, crossly, so it seemed, and in vexation, then flapped his hand and moved away.

I turned to him in fright, not understanding. There was the flash of someone else's eyes over my shoulder. Another doctor had come too.

Polyakov suddenly shifted his mouth crookedly, like someone feeling sleepy who wants to get rid of a persistent fly, and then his lower jaw started moving as though he were choking on a little lump of something and wanted to swallow it. Ah, anyone who has seen bad revolver or rifle wounds is very familiar with that movement! Maria Vlasyevna frowned painfully and sighed.

"Dr Bomgard," said Polyakov, barely audibly.

"I'm here," I whispered, and the sound of my voice was gentle, right beside his lips.

"The notebook's for you…" Polyakov responded, his voice hoarse and weaker still.

126

At that point he opened his eyes and raised them to the room's joyless ceiling, receding into darkness. His dark pupils began filling with light as though from within, and the whites of his eyes seemed to become transparent, bluish. His eyes came to a halt on high, then grew dull and lost that fleeting beauty.

Dr Polyakov was dead.

It's night. Close to dawn. The lamp burns very clearly, because the little town is sleeping and there's a lot of electric current. All is silent, and Polyakov's body is in the chapel. It's night.

On the desk in front of my eyes, which are sore from reading, lie an opened envelope and a sheet of paper.

On the latter is written:

Dear comrade!
I'm not going to wait for you. I've changed my mind about having treatment. It's hopeless. And I don't want to suffer any more either. I've had enough. I caution others: be careful with white crystals dissolved in twenty-five parts of water. I put too much trust in them and they have been my undoing. I'm giving you my diary. You always seemed to me an inquisitive man and a lover of human documents. If you're interested, read my medical record.
Farewell. Yours,
S. Polyakov.

A postscript in large letters:

Please don't blame anyone for my death.
Physician Sergei Polyakov.
13th February 1918.

Next to the suicide's letter is a notebook in black oilcloth, a sort of commonplace book. The first half of its pages has been torn out of it. In the remaining half there are short entries, at first in pencil or ink and in a small, precise hand, and at the end of the book in indelible pencil and a thick, red one and in a careless hand, a jumpy hand, and with a lot of abbreviated words.

IV

...7,[†] 20th January.

...and I'm very glad. And thank God, the more remote, the better. I can't bear to see anyone, and here I *shan't* see anyone, other than sick peasants. But they won't trouble my wound in any way, will they? Others, incidentally, have been planted out in zemstvo districts* much like me. My entire cohort of graduates, those not liable for call-up to the War (second category conscripts from 1916), have been distributed among the zemstvos. But that's of no interest to anyone. Of my friends, I've learnt only of Ivanov and Bomgard. Ivanov chose Archangel Province (a matter of taste), while Bomgard, as the female *feldsher* told me, is working in a remote district like mine, three districts away from me in Gorelovo. I was meaning to write to him, but changed my mind. I don't want to see or hear from anyone.

21st January.

A blizzard. Nothing.

25th January.

What a clear sunset. Migrainin – a combination of *antipirin, coffein** and *ac. citric.*

1.0 per powder... is 1.0 permissible? It is.

3rd February.

I received last week's newspapers today. I didn't start reading them, but was drawn, all the same, to have a look at the theatres section. *Aida* was on last week. That means

---

† Undoubtedly 1917 – *Dr Bomgard.*

129

she emerged onto a dais and sang: "Come, dearest friend, draw near to me…"*

She has an extraordinary voice, and how strange it is that a clear, huge voice has been given to a dark little soul…

[Here there is a break, two or three pages have been torn out.]

…of course it's unworthy, Dr Polyakov. And it's schoolboy stupidity to use the language of the marketplace to attack a woman because she's gone! She doesn't want to stay – she's gone. And that's an end to it. How simple it all is, in essence. An opera singer took up with a young doctor, stayed with him for a year, and now she's gone.

Kill her? Kill? Oh, how stupid, empty it all is. It's hopeless! I don't want to think. Don't want to…

11th February.

Blizzards and more blizzards… I'm being snowed in! For evenings on end I'm alone, alone. I light the lamp and sit there. In the daytime I do still see people. But I work mechanically. I've grown accustomed to the work. It's not as terrifying as I used to think. Actually, the military hospital in the War helped me a lot. I came here not entirely illiterate after all.

Today I performed the operation of version for the first time.

And so, there are three people buried here beneath the snow: me, Anna Kirillovna, who's a *feldsher* and midwife, and a male *feldsher*. He's married. They (the assistant staff) live in the wing. But I'm alone.

15th February.

Last night an interesting thing happened. I was getting ready for bed, when suddenly I had pains in the region of the stomach. But what pains! My forehead came out in a cold sweat. Our medicine is, after all, a dubious science, I have to say. What can make a man who has absolutely no ailment of the stomach or intestines (e.g. append.), who has a splendid liver and kidneys, whose intestines are functioning perfectly normally, have such pains in the night that he starts rolling around on his bed?

Groaning, I got as far as the kitchen, where the cook and her husband, Vlas, spend the nights. I sent Vlas to Anna Kirillovna. She came to me in the night and was forced to give me a morphine injection. She says I was absolutely green. Why?

I don't like our *feldsher*. He's unsociable, whereas Anna Kirillovna is a very nice and mature person. I'm amazed at how a woman of no age can live in complete solitude in this snowy coffin. Her husband is a prisoner of the Germans.

I cannot but give praise to the first man to extract morphine from poppy heads. A true benefactor of mankind. The pains ceased seven minutes after the injection. It's interesting: the pains were coming in one complete wave, without allowing any pauses, so that I was positively gasping for breath, as if someone were twisting a scorching crowbar that had been driven into my belly. Four minutes or so after the injection I began to discern an undulatory nature to the pain:

It would be a very good thing if a doctor had the opportunity of testing many a medicine on himself. He would have a completely different understanding of their effect. After the injection, for the first time in recent months I had a good, deep sleep – without any thoughts of the woman who deceived me.

16th February.

At surgery today Anna Kirillovna enquired how I felt, and said this was the first occasion in all this time that she'd seen me cheerful.

"Am I cheerless, then?"

"Very," she replied with conviction, and added that she was astounded by the fact that I was always silent.

"That's just the sort of man I am."

But that's a lie. I was a man full of *joie de vivre* until my domestic drama.

The dusk gathers early. I'm alone in the apartment. Pain came in the evening, but not great pain, like a shadow of yesterday's, somewhere behind my breastbone. Fearing the return of yesterday's attack, I injected one centigram into my thigh myself.

The pain ceased almost instantly. It's a good thing Anna Kirillovna left the phial.

18th.

Four injections are nothing to worry about.

25th February.

That Anna Kirillovna's an odd one! As though I'm not a doctor. 1½ syringes = 0.015 *morph.*? Yes.

1st March.

Dr Polyakov, be careful!

Nonsense.

Dusk.

But for already a couple of weeks now, my thoughts haven't once returned to the woman who deceived me. The motif from her role, Amneris, has left me. I'm very proud of this. I'm a man.

* * *

Anna K. has become my secret wife. It couldn't possibly have been otherwise. We're imprisoned on an uninhabited island.

The snow has changed, it seems to have become greyer. There are no more really hard frosts, but the blizzards do resume at times...

The first minute: a sensation of something touching my neck. This touch becomes warm and expands. In the second minute a cold wave suddenly passes through the pit of my stomach, and following that there begins an extraordinary clarification of my thought and an explosion of my capacity for work. Absolutely all unpleasant sensations cease. This is the high point of the manifestation of man's spiritual power. And if I hadn't been ruined by a medical education, I would have said that a man can only work properly after an injection of morphine. Truly: what damned use is a man if the slightest little neuralgia can completely knock him out of the saddle!

Anna K. is scared. I reassured her, saying that ever since I was a child I've been noted for the most enormous strength of will.

2nd March.

Rumours of something stupendous. Nicholas II has allegedly been toppled.*

I go to bed very early. At about nine o'clock. And sleep sweetly.

10th March.

There's a revolution going on there. The day has become longer, but the dusk seems to be a little bluer.

Never before have I had such dreams at dawn. They're double dreams.

What's more, the principal one, I'd say, is made of glass. It's transparent.

And so, then – I dream of an eerily lit lamp, and out of it blazes a multicoloured ribbon of lights. Amneris is waving a green feather and singing. The orchestra, utterly unearthly, is extraordinarily sonorous. I can't convey it in words, though. In short, in a normal dream music is soundless… (in a normal one? That's another question, which dream is more normal?! I'm joking, though…) soundless, but in *my* dream it's quite sublimely audible. And the main thing is that, using my will, I can amplify or soften the music. I seem to recall in *War and Peace* there's a description of how Petya Rostov, when half asleep, experienced the same state.* Leo Tolstoy's a remarkable writer!

Now about the transparency: so, then, showing completely realistically through the play of colours of Aida are the edge of my desk, which I can see from the door of the study, the lamp and the glossy floor, and bursting through the wave of the Bolshoi Theatre's orchestra I can hear clear footsteps, treading pleasantly like muffled castanets.

So it's eight o'clock, and this is Anna K. coming to my room to wake me up and tell me what's going on in the surgery.

She doesn't realize that I don't need waking, that I can hear everything and can talk to her.

And yesterday I did this experiment:

Anna – Sergei Vasilyevich…

I – I can hear… (*quietly to the music: "louder"*).

The music. – a grand chord. D sharp…

Anna – Twenty people have registered.

Amneris – (*sings*).

It can't be conveyed on paper though.

Are these dreams harmful? Oh no. After them I get up strong and in good spirits. And I work well. I'm even taking an interest now, whereas I wasn't before. And no wonder, all my thoughts were concentrated on my ex-wife.

But now I'm calm.

I'm calm.

19th March.

In the night I had a quarrel with Anna K.

"I'm not going to prepare the solution any more."

I started to try and persuade her.

"Nonsense, Annusya. What, a little boy, am I?"

"I'm not going to. You'll die."

"Well, as you wish. But you must understand that I've got pains in my chest!"

"Have treatment."

"Where?"

"Go away on leave. Morphine isn't treatment." (Then she had a think and added...) "I can't forgive myself for preparing the second bottle for you that time."

"What, I'm a morphine addict, am I?"

"Yes, you're becoming one."

"So you're not going to go?"

"No."

Here, for the first time, I discovered in myself an unpleasant capacity to get angry and, most importantly, shout at people when I'm in the wrong.

However, it wasn't at once. I went into the bedroom. Had a look. There was barely a splash at the bottom of the bottle. I drew it into a syringe – it proved to be a quarter full. I hurled the syringe down, almost breaking it, and started to tremble. Picked it up carefully and examined it – not a single crack. I sat in the bedroom for about twenty minutes. When I went out again, she wasn't there.

She'd gone.

Imagine – I couldn't bear it, I went to see her. I knocked at the lighted window in her wing. She came out onto the porch wrapped up in a scarf. The night was ever so quiet. The snow fluffy. Somewhere far away in the sky there was a breath of spring.

"Anna Kirillovna, be so good as to give me the keys to the pharmacy."

She whispered:

"No, I won't."

"Comrade, be so good as to give me the keys to the pharmacy. I'm speaking to you as a doctor."

I could see in the dusk that her face altered, she turned very white, while her eyes deepened, sank, turned black. And she replied in a voice that made pity stir in my soul.

But straight away anger surged over me again.

She:

"Why do you talk like that, why? Ah, Sergei Vasilyevich, I'm acting out of pity for you."

And at this point she freed her hands from under the scarf, and I could see that she had the keys in her hands. So she had come out to me and brought them with her.

I (rudely):

"Give me the keys!"

I tore them out of her hands.

And I set off over the rotten, bouncing planked footway towards the white building of the hospital.

Fury was sizzling in my soul, first and foremost because I have absolutely no idea at all of how to prepare a morphine solution for subcutaneous injection. I'm a doctor, not a *feldsher*!

I shook as I walked.

And I could hear that, behind me, like a faithful dog, she had set off too. And tenderness shot up inside me, but I suppressed it. I turned and, baring my teeth, said:

136

"Are you going to do it or not?"

And she flapped a hand like someone doomed, as if to say "it's all the same", and answered quietly:

"Let me do it…"

…An hour later I was in a reasonable state. Of course, I begged her pardon for my senseless rudeness. I didn't know myself what had come over me. I used to be a polite person before.

Her response to my apology was strange. She went down on her knees, pressed herself up against my hands and said:

"I'm not cross with you. No. I already know now that you're done for. I know it. And I curse myself for having given you the injection that time."

I calmed her as best I could, assuring her that she was absolutely nothing to do with this and that I myself was answerable for my actions. I promised her that from tomorrow I would seriously begin breaking the habit by decreasing the dose.

"How much have you just injected?"

"A silly amount. Three syringes of one-per cent solution."

She took her head in her hands and fell silent.

"Don't you worry!"

…In essence, I can understand her anxiety. *Morphinum hydrochloricum* is, indeed, a formidable thing. The habit for it forms very quickly. But a little habit isn't morphine addiction, is it?…

…To tell the truth, that woman is the only person who is genuinely faithful to me. And in essence, she really ought to be my wife. I've forgotten the other one. Forgotten her. And for that, after all, it's thank you to the morphine…

8th April 1917.

It's agony.

137

9th April.
   The spring is dreadful.

The Devil in a bottle. Cocaine is the Devil in a bottle.
   This is its effect:
   Almost instantly after injecting one syringeful of two-per cent solution, a state of calm sets in which turns straight away into delight and bliss. But this continues for only one or two minutes. And then it's all lost without trace, as if it had never been. Pain, dread, darkness set in. The spring roars, black birds fly from bare branch to bare branch, while in the distance the forest reaches towards the sky like bristles, broken and black, and beyond it, encompassing a quarter of the sky, there burns the first sunset of spring.
   I pace the big, lonely, empty room in the doctor's apart- ment diagonally, from the doors to the window and from the window to the doors. How many such walks can I take? Fifteen or sixteen – no more. And then I have to turn and go into the bedroom. The syringe is lying on some gauze next to the bottle. I pick it up and, carelessly rubbing some iodine onto my thigh, which is covered in needle marks, I plunge the needle into my skin. There's no pain. Oh, on the contrary: I'm anticipating the euphoria that will soon be coming. And then it does come. I know of it because the sounds of the accordion which Vlas the watchman, rejoic- ing at spring, is playing on the porch, the ragged, hoarse sounds of the accordion, which come flying to me, muffled, through the window pane, become angelic voices, and the rough basses in billowing furs hum like a heavenly choir. But then, after an instant, obeying some mysterious law which isn't described in a single one of the pharmacology books, the cocaine in the blood is transformed into something new. I know: it's a mixture of the Devil and my blood. And on the porch Vlas flags, and I hate him, while the sunset, with

an uneasy rumbling, scorches my innards. And that's how it is several times running in the course of an evening until I realize that I'm poisoned. My heart starts thumping such that I can feel it in my arms, in my temples... and then it sinks into an abyss, and there are sometimes moments when I think that Dr Polyakov won't come back to life again...

13th April.

I – the unfortunate Dr Polyakov, who in February of this year fell ill with morphine addiction – warn all those to whose lot a fate such as mine falls not to try substituting cocaine for morphine. Cocaine is the most horrible and insidious poison. Yesterday Anna barely nursed me back with camphor, and today I'm a semi-corpse...

6th May 1917.

I haven't touched my diary in quite a long time. And that's a pity. In essence, it isn't a diary but a medical record, and I evidently feel professionally drawn to my only friend in the world (if you don't count my mournful and often tearful friend Anna).

And so, if I'm to write a medical record, then here: I'm injecting myself with morphine twice a day, at five o'clock in the afternoon (after dinner) and at twelve midnight, before going to bed.

A three-per cent solution: two syringefuls. Consequently, I'm getting 0.06 at a time.

Quite a bit!

My earlier notes were somewhat hysterical. There's nothing in particular to worry about. It doesn't affect my capacity for work at all. On the contrary, I live all day on the nocturnal injection of the day before. I manage operations magnificently, I'm irreproachably attentive to the principles of prescription-writing, and give my word as a doctor that my morphine addiction has done my patients no harm. But there's something else that's tormenting me. It constantly seems to me that somebody will find out about my vice. And I find it difficult during surgery, feeling the hard, searching gaze of my assistant *feldsher* on my back.

Nonsense! He hasn't guessed. Nothing gives me away. It's only in the evening that my pupils might betray me, but I never encounter him in the evening.

I've replenished the quite awful depletion of morphine in our pharmacy after a trip to the local town. But even there I had to endure some unpleasant moments. The manager of the store took my order, in which I had also prudently included all sorts of other nonsense like caffeine (of which we have as much as you like), and said:

"Forty grams of morphine?"

And I sense that I'm averting my eyes like a schoolboy. I sense that I'm blushing...

He says:

"We don't have such a quantity. I'll give you ten grams or so."

And he *doesn't* have it, it's true, but it seems to me that he has penetrated my secret, that his eyes are probing and drilling into me, and I am agitated and suffering.

No, it's the pupils, only the pupils that are dangerous, and for that reason I shall make it a rule not to encounter people in the evening. In that respect, incidentally, a more convenient place than my district couldn't be found; I haven't seen anyone but my patients for more than six months now. And I'm absolutely nothing to them.

18th May.

It's a stuffy night. There's going to be a storm. The black belly in the distance beyond the forest is growing and swelling. And there it is, a pale and alarming flash. The storm's coming.

There's a book in front of my eyes, and it says in it, regarding abstinence from morphine:

> ...great anxiety, a state of disquiet and depression, irritability, deterioration of the memory, sometimes hallucinations and, to a limited extent, blackouts...

I haven't experienced hallucinations, but regarding the remainder I can say: oh, what tame, banal words, words that say nothing!

"A state of depression"!...

No, having fallen ill with this dreadful illness, I warn doctors to be more compassionate towards their patients. It's not "a state of depression", but a slow death that takes hold of a morphine addict, as soon as you deprive him of morphine for an hour or two. The air is insubstantial, it can't be swallowed... there isn't a cell in the body that doesn't thirst... For what? That can be neither defined nor explained. In short, the man is gone. He's switched off. It's a corpse that moves, yearns, suffers. He wants nothing, thinks about nothing but morphine. Morphine!

Death from thirst is a heavenly, blissful one in comparison with the thirst for morphine. This is probably the way someone buried alive tries to catch the last, insignificant little air bubbles in the coffin and tears the skin on his chest with his nails. This is the way a heretic at the stake groans and stirs when the first tongues of flame lick at his feet...

Death – a dry, slow death...

That's what lies beneath those professorial words "a state of depression".

* * *

I can't go on. And so I've just gone and injected myself. A deep breath. Another deep breath.

That's better. But now… now… there's the minty chill in the pit of my stomach…

Three syringefuls of a three-per cent solution. That'll last me until midnight…

Rubbish. That entry is rubbish. It's not so terrible. Sooner or later I'll give it up!… But now I've got to sleep, sleep.

I'm simply tormenting and weakening myself with this silly struggle with morphine.

[Hereafter a couple of dozen pages have been cut out of the notebook.]

…ber

…ain vomiting at 4.30.

When I'm feeling better I'll note down my dreadful impressions.

14th November 1917.

And so, after fleeing from Dr …'s [the name has been thoroughly crossed out] clinic in Moscow, I'm at home again. The rain is pouring down in sheets and hiding the world from me. And let it hide it from me. I don't need it, just as no one in the world needs me. I lived through shooting and revolt while I was in the clinic. But the idea of giving up the treatment had furtively ripened inside me even before the fighting on the streets of Moscow. Thank you, morphine, for making me brave. I'm not afraid of any shooting. And what is there in general that can frighten a man who thinks of only one thing – of the wonderful, divine crystals. When the *feldsher*, completely terrorized by the booming of cannons…

[Here a page has been torn out.]

...rn out this page so that nobody would read the shameful description of the way a man with a degree fled furtively, like a coward, and stole his own suit.

The suit – that's nothing!

I took a hospital shirt. There were other things on my mind. The next day, after having an injection, I came back to life and returned to Dr N. He greeted me compassionately, but there was contempt showing through the compassion all the same. And that was wrong. After all, he's a psychiatrist, and he ought to understand that I'm not always in control of myself. I'm ill. Why should he feel contempt for me? I returned the hospital shirt.

He said:

"Thank you," and added: "What are you thinking of doing now?"

I said cheerily (at that moment I was in a state of euphoria):

"I've decided to go back to my place in the backwoods, particularly as my leave has run out. I'm very grateful to you for your help, I feel significantly better. I'll continue the treatment at home."

This was his reply:

"You don't feel a bit better. I really do find it funny that you can say that to me. I mean, just one look at your pupils is enough. Who do you think you're talking to?..."

"I can't break the habit all at once, Professor... now in particular, when all these events are taking place... the shooting has completely unnerved me..."

"It's over. There's a new regime. Come back into the clinic."

At that point I remembered everything... the cold corridors... the empty walls, painted with oil paints... and I'm crawling like a dog with a broken leg... waiting for something... What? A hot bath?... An injection of 0.005 of morphine. A dose of which no one dies, it's true... but only… yet all the depression remains, it lies like a burden, just as it did before… The empty nights, the shirt I was wearing and ripped to pieces, begging to be let out?…

No. No. Morphine was invented, it was extracted from the dried, rattling heads of a divine plant, so find a way of treating people without tormenting them too! I shook my head stubbornly. At this point he started to rise, and I suddenly flung myself towards the door in fright. I thought he wanted to lock the door behind me and keep me in the clinic by force…

The Professor turned crimson.

"I'm not a prison governor," he said, not without irritation, "and this isn't Butyrki.* Sit quietly. You were boasting that you were completely normal two weeks ago. And yet…" – he expressively repeated my gesture of fright – "I'm not holding you here, sir."

"Professor, give me back the paper I signed. I beg of you," and my voice even had a pitiful quaver to it.

"Certainly."

He gave a click with a key in the desk and gave me back the document I had signed (about my pledging to follow the entire two-month course of treatment, and their being able to detain me at the clinic, etc., in short, of the usual kind).

I took the note with a trembling hand and put it away, murmuring:

"Thank you."

Then I stood up to leave. And started to go.

"Dr Polyakov!" rang out in my wake. I turned, holding on to the door handle. "Look here," he began, "think again. You must understand that you'll find yourself back in the psychiatric clinic all the same, albeit a little later on… And, what's more, you'll be in a much worse state. I've been dealing with you as with a doctor, after all. But when you come back then, you'll already be in a state of complete mental collapse. Essentially, my friend, you shouldn't be practising, and it's probably criminal not to notify your place of work."

I winced and felt distinctly that the colour had drained from my face (though I have very little of it to begin with).

"I beg you, Professor," I said in a muffled voice, "not to say anything to anyone... Why, I'll be dismissed... stigmatized as a sick man... Why would you want to do that to me?"

"Go," he cried in vexation, "go. I won't say anything. You'll be sent back all the same..."

I left, and I swear I was twitching in pain and shame for the entire journey... Why?...

It's very simple. Ah, my friend, my faithful diary. You won't give me away, will you? It isn't a matter of the suit, but of my stealing morphine at the clinic. Three cubic centimetres in crystals and ten grams of one-per cent solution.

That's not the only thing that interests me, there's this too. The key was sticking out of the cabinet. Well, and what if it hadn't been there? Would I have forced the cabinet open or not? Eh? If I'm honest?

Yes, I would.

And so, Dr Polyakov is a thief. There'll be ample time for me to tear the page out.

Well, as regards my practising though, he did go too far. Yes, I'm a degenerate. Absolutely true. The disintegration of my moral being has started. But I can work, I can't do any evil or harm to any of my patients.

Yes, why did I steal? It's very simple. I decided that during the fighting and all the commotion connected with the revolt, I wouldn't get hold of any morphine anywhere. But when it calmed down, I got hold of another fifteen grams of one-per cent solution in a chemist's on the outskirts of town – which for me is useless and tedious (I'll have to inject nine syringefuls!). And I had to demean myself too. The pharmacist demanded an official stamp, and the looks he gave me were sullen and suspicious. But on the other hand, the next day, when back to normal, I got twenty grams in crystals at another chemist's without any delay at all – wrote an order for the hospital (and at the same time, of course, ordered caffeine and aspirin). Yes, when all's said and done, why should I hide and be afraid? Indeed, as though I had it written on my forehead that I'm a morphine addict? Whose business is it, when all's said and done?

And is the disintegration so great? I adduce these diary entries as witnesses. They're fragmented, but after all, I'm not a writer! There aren't any crazy ideas in them, are there? I think my reasoning is perfectly sound.

A morphine addict has one piece of good fortune, which nobody can take away from him – the capacity to spend his life in total solitude. And solitude means important, significant ideas, it means contemplation, tranquillity, wisdom...

The night flows by, black and silent. Somewhere out there is the forest, stripped bare, and beyond it are the river, cold, autumn.

Far, far away is dishevelled, turbulent Moscow. I don't care about anything, I don't need anything, and I'm not drawn to go anywhere.

Burn, light, inside my lamp, burn quietly, I want to rest after the adventures of Moscow, I want to forget them.

And I have.

I have.

18th November.

Light frosts. It's dried up. I went out for a walk down the path towards the river, because I hardly ever get a breath of air.

Even if my being is disintegrating, I'm making attempts, all the same, to abstain from it. This morning, for example, I didn't do any injecting. (I'm now injecting three syringefuls of four-per cent solution three times a day.) It's awkward. I'm sorry for Anna. Every new per cent is killing her. I'm sorry. Oh, what a person!

Yes… right… so… when I began to feel bad, I decided nonetheless to torment myself a bit (if only Professor N. could see me) by delaying the injection, and I set off towards the river.

What a wilderness. Not a sound, not a rustle. There's no dusk yet, but it's there somewhere, hiding, and it's creeping over the marshes, over the hummocks, between the tree stumps… It's coming, coming to the Levkovo Hospital… And I'm creeping along, leaning on a stick (to tell the truth, I've grown somewhat weaker of late).

And then I see that, flying swiftly up the slope from the river towards me, without moving her legs beneath her many-coloured bell-shaped skirt, is a little old woman with yellow hair… For the first few moments I didn't understand who she was and wasn't even frightened. A little old woman like any other. Strange – why is the old woman bareheaded and wearing only a blouse in the cold?… And then: where's the old woman from? Who is she? When our surgery at Levkovo is over and the last peasants' sledges go their different ways, there's no one for ten versts all around. Mists, marshes, forests! And then suddenly cold sweat started running down my back – I understood! The little old woman wasn't running, but actually *flying*, not touching the ground. Nice? Yet that wasn't the thing that tore a cry from me, but the fact that

147

in the old woman's hands there was a pitchfork. Why was I so frightened? Why? I fell onto one knee, holding my hands out, shielding myself, so as not to see her, then I turned and, hobbling, ran towards home, as to a place of salvation, not wishing for anything other than for my heart not to burst, and for my soon to be running into warm rooms and seeing Anna alive... and for morphine...

And I ran back.

Nonsense. A trivial hallucination. A chance hallucination.

19th November.
Vomiting. This is bad.

My nocturnal conversation with Anna on the 21st.

Anna – The *feldsher* knows.

I – Really? I don't care. It's nothing.

Anna – If you don't leave here and go to town, I'll hang myself. Do you hear? Look at your hands, look at them.

I – They're trembling a little. It doesn't prevent me from working at all.

Anna – Will you look – they're transparent. Just bone and skin... Take a look at your face... Listen, Seryozha. Go away, I implore you, go away...

I – What about you?

Anna – Go away. Go away. You're dying.

I – Well, that's overstating it. But I really can't understand myself why I've grown weak so quickly. After all, I haven't been ill for a full year yet. It's evidently my constitution.

Anna (sadly) – What can bring you back to life? Perhaps that Amneris of yours – your wife?

I – Oh no. You can relax. Thank you to the morphine, it rid me of her. Instead of her there's morphine.

Anna – Oh my God... what am I going to do?

* * *

I thought there were people like Anna only in novels. And if I ever recover, I shall throw in my lot with her for good. May the other not return from Germany.

27th December.

I haven't picked up my notebook in a long time. I'm all wrapped up, and the horses are waiting. Bomgard has gone from the Gorelovo district, and I've been sent to replace him. A woman doctor's coming to my district.

Anna's here… She'll come and visit me…

Even if it is thirty versts.

We've come to a firm decision that from 1st January I shall take a month's sick leave and go to the Professor in Moscow. I'll sign another document, and I'll suffer a month of inhuman torment at his clinic.

Farewell, Levkovo. Anna, goodbye.

1918.

January.

I didn't go. I can't part with my crystalline, soluble idol. I shall die during treatment.

And it occurs to me more and more often that I don't *need* treatment.

15th January.

Vomiting in the morning.

Three syringefuls of four-per cent solution at dusk.

Three syringefuls of four-per cent solution in the night.

16th January.

An operating day, and so great abstinence – from the night until six o'clock in the evening.

At dusk – the most dreadful time – when already in my apartment, I distinctly heard a voice, monotonous and menacing, repeating:

"Sergei Vasilyevich. Sergei Vasilyevich."

After injecting, it all faded away at once.

17th January.

There's a blizzard – no surgery. During abstinence I read a psychiatry textbook and it made a horrifying impression on me. I'm done for, there's no hope.

During abstinence, I'm frightened of rustling noises, people are hateful to me. I'm afraid of them. During the euphoria I love them all, but I prefer solitude.

Here I have to be cautious – there's a *feldsher* and two midwives here. I have to be very careful so as not to give myself away. I've become experienced, and won't do so. No one will find out while I have a supply of morphine. I prepare solutions myself or send a prescription to Anna well in advance. Once she made an attempt (an absurd one) to substitute a two-per cent solution for a five-per cent one. She brought it from Levkovo herself in freezing cold and a snowstorm.

And we had a serious quarrel because of it during the night. I convinced her not to do it. I've informed the staff here that I'm ill. I racked my brains for a long time over what illness to invent. I said I had rheumatic legs and severe neurasthenia. They've been notified that I'm going on leave to Moscow in February for treatment. Things are going smoothly. There have been no failures at work. I avoid operating on the days when I start having uncontrolled vomiting and hiccups. And so I had to give myself intestinal catarrh as well. Ah, that's too many illnesses in a single man!

The staff here are compassionate and are themselves urging me to go on leave.

150

* * *

External appearance: thin, and pale with a waxen pallor.

I took a bath and at the same time weighed myself on the hospital scales. Last year I weighed four poods, and now three poods, fifteen pounds.* I took fright when I looked at the arrow, but it passed.

There are incessant boils on my forearms, and the same on my thighs. I don't know how to prepare sterile solutions, and apart from that I injected myself two or three times with a syringe that hadn't been boiled, I was in a great hurry before the journey.

That's inadmissible.

18th January.

I had the following hallucination:

I'm expecting pale people of some sort to appear at the black windows. It's unbearable. There's only one blind. I got some gauze from the hospital and hung it as a curtain. I couldn't think up a pretext.

Oh, damn it! Why, when all's said and done, do I have to think up a pretext for my every action? I mean, it really is torment, not a life!

Am I expressing my thoughts smoothly? I think I am.
A life? Ridiculous!

19th January.

In an interval during surgery today, while we were relaxing and smoking in the pharmacy, the *feldsher*, twisting the powders around, told (for some reason laughing) of how a female *feldsher* suffering from morphine addiction, who had no opportunity to get hold of any morphine, used to take half a glass of laudanum. I didn't know where to look during this agonizing story. What's funny in that? It's hateful to me. What's funny about it? What?

I left the pharmacy with the gait of a thief.

"What do you find funny about this affliction?..."

But I restrained myself, restra—

In my situation it doesn't do to be particularly haughty with people.

Ah, the *feldsher*. He's just as cruel as those psychiatrists, who don't know how to help a sick man at all.

Not at all.

Not at all.

The preceding lines were written during abstinence, and there's a lot in them that's unfair.

It's a moonlit night now. I'm lying down, weak after an attack of vomiting. I can't lift my arms up high and I'm jotting my thoughts down in pencil. They're pure and proud. For a few hours I'm happy. Ahead of me is sleep. Above me is the moon, and on it there's a crown. Nothing's to be feared after an injection.

1st February.

Anna's come. She's yellow, sick.

I've finished her off. Finished her off. Yes, there's a great sin on my conscience.

I swore to her that I was leaving in the middle of February.

Will I keep my word?

Yes. I will.

If I'm alive.

3rd February.

And so. A hill. Icy and endless, like the one from which the fairy-tale character Kay was taken by the sledge as a child.* My last flight down that hill, and I know what awaits me at the bottom.

Oh, Anna, there'll soon be great sorrow for you, if you loved me...

11th February.

This is what I've decided. I'll appeal to Bomgard. Why him specifically? Because he's not a psychiatrist, because he's young and a university comrade. He's healthy and strong, but gentle, if I'm right. I remember him. Maybe he'll be... I'll find sympathy in him. He'll think of something. Let him take me to Moscow. I can't go to him. I've already had leave. I'm in bed. I don't go to the hospital.

I slandered the *feldsher*. He laughed, so what... It's not important. He came to see me. Offered to listen to me.

I didn't let him. More pretexts for the refusal? I don't want to think up a pretext.

The note to Bomgard has been sent.

People! Will someone help me?

I've started emotional exclamations. And if anyone were to read this, they'd think it insincere. But no one will.

Before writing to Bomgard, I ran through everything in my mind. What came up in particular was the station in Moscow in November when I was fleeing from Moscow. What a dreadful evening. I was injecting stolen morphine in a lavatory... It's torment. They were trying to force their way in, there's the thundering of voices like iron, they're cursing me for keeping the place engaged for a long time, and my hands are jerking, and the catch is jerking, the next thing you know, the door'll fly open...

It's since then I've had furuncles.

I cried in the night at the memory of it.

12th, during the night.

And cr. again. Why this weakness and loathsomeness during the night?

1918. 13th February at dawn in Gorelovka.

I can congratulate myself: I've already gone fourteen hours without an injection! It's an unthinkable figure. Day is breaking, turbid and whitish. Will I be perfectly well now?

On second thoughts: I don't need Bomgard, nor anyone else. It would be shameful to extend my life even for a minute. A life like this – no, I mustn't. I have medicine to hand. Why didn't I think of it before?

Well, let's make a start. I don't owe anyone anything. I've destroyed only myself. And Anna. What can I do?

Time will heal, as Amner. used to sing. Where she's concerned, of course, it's straightforward and simple.

The notebook goes to Bomgard. That's it...

V

A T DAWN ON 14TH February 1918 in a distant little town I read these, Sergei Polyakov's diary entries. And here they are in full, without any alterations whatsoever. I'm not a psychiatrist, I can't say with certainty whether they're instructive, whether they're needed. I think they are needed.

Now, when ten years have passed, the pity and fear elicited by the entries have, of course, gone. That's natural, but, having reread these notes now, when Polyakov's body has long rotted away, and all memory of him has disappeared, I have kept an interest in him. Maybe they are needed? I make so bold as to come to an affirmative decision. Anna K. died of typhus in 1922 in that same rural district where she worked. Amneris – Polyakov's first wife – is abroad. And won't return.

Can I publish these notes, given to me as a gift?

I can. I'm publishing them. Dr Bomgard.

Autumn 1927

Note on the Texts

The texts used for this translation were those in Vol. II of M.A. Bulgakov, *Sobranie sochinenii v vos'mi tomakh* (Moscow: AST-Astrel', 2008). The seven stories that make up the cycle *A Young Doctor's Notebook* were never published together during the author's lifetime, but they did all appear in the years 1925–26 in the periodical *Meditsinskii rabotnik* (*The Medical Worker*), with the sole exception of 'The Steel Throat', which was published in *Krasnaia panorama* (*Red Panorama*) in 1925. The longer story 'Morphine' was also published in *Meditsinskii rabotnik*, albeit slightly later, in 1927, and has clear associations with the other tales in this collection, through, for example, the narrative voice of the frame and the tale's setting. The fact that the stories were all originally published as separate entities accounts for the small degree of repetition in them (e.g. the presentation of the narrator's colleagues, the description of the layout of the doctor's apartment), and also for certain inconsistencies, particularly in the naming of the narrator's rural hospital – Murye, Muryevo, Muryino, Nikolskoye, Gorelovo, Gorelovka – and also in the chronology. The inconsistencies have been retained in this English translation.

Notes

p. 3, *the forty versts*: A verst was a Russian measure of length approximately equivalent to one kilometre.

p. 3, *Muryino Hospital*: The name of the narrator's rural hospital varies across the several stories. This is because the stories were originally published separately. See the Note on the Texts for more information.

p. 4, *feldsher's*: A *feldsher* (from the German Feldscher, an army surgeon) was originally in the eighteenth century an assistant to a military surgeon in the field, but by the twentieth century had become an essential element in Russia's medical system, especially in rural areas, as a trained assistant to a doctor.

p. 4, *Greetings to you... my sa-cred re-fuge*: The opening of the eponymous hero's aria from Act III of the opera *Faust* (1859) by Charles Gounod (1818–93).

p. 9, *the False Dmitry*: Grigory Otrepyev became the figurehead for the opposition to the rule of Boris Godunov in 1604, when he claimed to be Dmitry, a son of Ivan the Terrible believed to have been killed in 1591. He was hailed as tsar after Godunov's death in 1605, but was deposed and killed the following year.

p. 10, *natrii salicylici... infusum*: *Natrii salicylici* is sodium salicylate, commonly used as a painkiller and to reduce fever. "*Infusum*" is the Latin for "infusion": the narrator is considering preparing a remedy by soaking the roots of the flower *Cephaelis ipecacuanha*, a common emetic.

p. 11, *you ill-starred Aesculapius*: In Greek mythology, Aesculapius, a son of Apollo, the god of medicine, was himself a healer and physician who became a demigod.

p. 12, *plica polonica*: "Polish plait" (Latin). A condition caused when poorly cared-for hair becomes so enmeshed that it forms a single matted lump.

p. 16, *clicking the Collin*: I.e. a surgical-needle holder manufactured by the French surgical-instrument makers Collin.

p. 21, *Esmarch mug*: A vessel named after a German military surgeon J.F.A. von Esmarch (1823–1908).

p. 23, *Döderlein*: The German gynaecologist Albert Döderlein (1860–1941).

p. 23, *Podalic version*: A procedure whereby the foetus is manually turned within the womb.

p. 43, *Now it cries, just like a child*: Lines from the poem 'A Winter's Evening' (1825) by Alexander Pushkin (1799–1837).

p. 49, *of the time of Nicholas I*: The Emperor Nicholas I (b.1796) ruled Russia from 1825 until his death in 1855.

p. 55, *Leo Tolstoy… Yasnaya Polyana*: Yasnaya Polyana was the family estate on which Leo Tolstoy (1828–1910) spent much of his life; the reference to Tolstoy may relate to the story 'Master and Man' (1895), in which the protagonists get lost in a blizzard, or 'The Snowstorm' (1856). The narrator's plight is, quite naturally, not uncommon in Russian literature generally.

p. 61, *Egyptian Darkness*: The phrase alludes to Exodus 10:21–23 and is a metaphor for the ignorance of the Russian peasantry.

p. 80, *Lues III*: "Lues" is another term for syphilis. The Roman numerals indicate that this is the tertiary stage.

p. 91, *a five-gram Luer*: A glass syringe named after the nineteenth-century German medical-instrument maker Hermann Luer.

p. 91, *salvarsan*: A drug used to treat syphilis.

p. 93, *an Englishman who landed up on an uninhabited island*: The reference is to the story 'The Life of Gnor' (1912) by Alexander Grin, the pen name of Alexander Stefanovich Grinevsky (1880–1932).

p. 96, *A book in a yellow binding with the inscription Sakhalin*: The reference is to the book *Sakhalin (Penal Servitude)* (1903) by the journalist Vlas Mikhailovich Doroshevich (1864–1922), which describes the penal colony found on Sakhalin Island, located in the North Pacific off Russia's eastern coast.

p. 97, *Fenimore Cooper's The Pathfinder*: The novel of 1840 by the American writer James Fenimore Cooper (1789–1851). Set in America during the Seven Years War between the French and the British, it is fourth in the five-novel series known as *The Leatherstocking Tales*, about the adventures of Natty Bumppo, a child of white parents raised by Native Americans.

p. 101, *Chekhov story… sexton having a tooth pulled*: The reference is to the story 'Surgery' (1884) by another of Russia's doctor-writers, Anton Pavlovich Chekhov (1860–1904).

p. 103, *Kerensky*: Alexander Fyodorovich Kerensky (1881–1970) was Minister for Justice and Minister for War before heading the Provisional Government after the February Revolution of 1917; he was forced to flee abroad after the Bolsheviks seized power in the October Revolution.

p. 105, *How many fives… He put a three against my name*: In the Russian education system a five was the top mark, signifying "excellent"; a three signified merely "satisfactory".

p. 113, *happy in 1917*: The chronology in this story is noticeably inconsistent with that of the earlier tales. This is again due to the fact that the stories were originally published separately. See the Note on the Texts for more information.

p. 113, *the local Basile*: Barbers in Russia at this time would often have their names written on their shop signs in the French manner to emphasize their pretensions to chic.

p. 118, *pyramidon*: A drug used to relieve pain and reduce fever.

p. 129, *zemstvo districts*: A zemstvo was a district or provincial assembly with certain local administrative powers.

p. 129, *antipirin, coffein*: I.e. antipyrin, a drug used to combat fever, and caffeine.

p. 130, *Come, dearest friend, draw near to me*: A line sung by Amneris, the Pharoah's daughter, to Aida, the captured Ethiopian princess who is Amneris's rival for the affections of the soldier Radames, in Act I of the opera *Aida* (1871) by Giuseppe Verdi (1813–1901).

p. 133, *Nicholas II has allegedly been toppled*: Nicholas II's document of abdication was signed on 2nd March in the Old Style (Julian) calendar in use in Russia in 1917.

p. 134, *Petya Rostov... experienced the same state*: The passage referred to is in Volume IV, Part III, chapter 10 of Tolstoy's novel.

p. 144, *this isn't Butyrki*: The name of Moscow's most infamous prison.

p. 151, *three poods fifteen pounds*: A pood was a Russian unit of weight equivalent to approximately sixteen kilograms.

p. 153, *fairy-tale character Kay was taken by the sledge as a child*: The reference is to the 'The Snow Queen' (1845) by Hans Christian Andersen (1805–75).

Extra Material

on

Mikhail Bulgakov's

A Young Doctor's Notebook

Mikhail Bulgakov's Life

Mikhail Afanasyevich Bulgakov was born in Kiev – then in the Russian Empire, now the capital of independent Ukraine – on 15th May 1891. He was the eldest of seven children – four sisters and three brothers – and, although born in Ukraine, his family were Russians, and were all members of the educated classes – mainly from the medical, teaching and ecclesiastical professions. His grandfathers were both Russian Orthodox priests, while his father lectured at Kiev Theological Academy. Although a believer, he was never fanatical, and he encouraged his children to read as widely as they wished, and to make up their own minds on everything. His mother was a teacher and several of his uncles were doctors.

Birth, Family Background and Education

In 1906 his father became ill with sclerosis of the kidneys. The Theological Academy immediately awarded him a full pension, even though he had not completed the full term of service, and allowed him to retire on health grounds. However, he died almost immediately afterwards.

Every member of the Bulgakov family played a musical instrument, and Mikhail became a competent pianist. There was an excellent repertory company and opera house in Kiev, which he visited regularly. He was already starting to write plays which were performed by the family in their drawing room. He was a conservative and a monarchist in his school days, but never belonged to any of the extreme right-wing organizations of the time. Like many of his contemporaries, he favoured the idea of a constitutional monarchy as against Russian Tsarist autocracy.

A few years after her first husband's death, Mikhail's mother married an uncompromising atheist. She gave the children supplementary lessons in her spare time from her own teaching job and, as soon as they reached adolescence, she encouraged them to take on younger pupils to increase the family's meagre income. Mikhail's first job, undertaken when he was still at school, was as a part-time guard and ticket inspector on the local railway,

165

and he continued such part-time employment when he entered medical school in Kiev in 1911.

He failed the exams at the end of his first year, but passed the resits a few months later. However, he then had to repeat his entire second year; this lack of dedication to his studies was possibly due to the fact that he was already beginning to write articles for various student journals and to direct student theatricals. Furthermore, he was at this time courting Tatyana Lappa, whom he married in 1913. She came from the distant Saratov region, but had relatives in Kiev, through whom she became acquainted with Bulgakov. He had already begun by this time to write short stories and plays. Because of these distractions, Bulgakov took seven years to complete what was normally a five-year course, but he finally graduated as a doctor in 1916 with distinction.

War   In 1914 the First World War had broken out, and Bulgakov enlisted immediately after graduation as a Red Cross volunteer, working in military hospitals at the front, which involved carrying out operations. In March 1916 he was called up to the army, but was in the end sent to work in a major Kiev hospital to replace experienced doctors who had been mobilized earlier. His wife, having done a basic nursing course by this time, frequently worked alongside her husband.

In March 1917 the Tsar abdicated, and the Russian monarchy collapsed. Two forces then began to contend for power – the Bolsheviks and the Ukrainian Nationalists. Although not completely in control of Ukraine, the latter declared independence from the former Tsarist Empire in February 1918, and concluded a separate peace deal with Germany. The Germans engineered a coup, placed their own supporters at the helm in Ukraine and supported this puppet regime against the Bolsheviks, the now deposed Nationalists and various other splinter groups fighting for their own causes. The Government set up its own German-supported army, the White Guard, which provided the background for Bulgakov's novel of the same name. The Bolsheviks ("The Reds"), the White Guard ("The Whites") and the Ukrainian Nationalists regularly took and retook the country and Kiev from each other: there were eighteen changes of government between the beginning of 1918 and late 1919.

Early in this period Bulgakov had been transferred to medical service in the countryside around the remote town of Vyazma, which provided him with material for his series of short stories

A Young Doctor's Notebook. Possibly to blunt the distress caused to him by the suffering he witnessed there, and to cure fevers he caught from the peasants he was tending, he dosed himself heavily on his own drugs, and rapidly became addicted to morphine. When his own supplies had run out, he sent his wife to numerous pharmacies to pick up new stocks for imaginary patients. When she finally refused to acquiesce in this any further, he became abusive and violent, and even threatened her with a gun. No more mention is made at any later date of his addiction, so it is uncertain whether he obtained professional help for the problem or weaned himself off his drug habit by his own will-power.

He returned to Kiev in February 1918 and set up in private practice. Some of the early stories written in this period show that he was wrestling with problems of direction and conscience: a doctor could be pressed into service by whichever faction was in power at that moment; after witnessing murders, torture and pogroms, Bulgakov was overwhelmed with horror at the contemporary situation. He was press-ganged mainly by the right-wing Whites, who were notoriously anti-Semitic and carried out most of the pogroms.

Perhaps as a result of the suffering he had seen during his enforced military service, he suffered a "spiritual crisis" – as an acquaintance of his termed it – in February 1920, when he gave up medicine at the age of twenty-nine to devote himself to literature. But things were changing in the literary world: Bulgakov's style and motifs were not in tune with the new proletarian values which the Communists, in the areas where they had been victorious, were already beginning to inculcate. The poet Anna Akhmatova talked of his "magnificent contempt" for their ethos, in which everything had to be subordinated to the creation of a new, optimistic mentality which believed that science, medicine and Communism would lead to a paradise on earth for all, with humanity reaching its utmost point of development.

Turning to Literature

He continued to be pressed into service against his will. Although not an ardent right-winger, he had more sympathy for the Whites than for the Reds, and when the former, who had forced him into service at the time, suffered a huge defeat at the hands of the Communists, evidence suggests that Bulgakov would rather have retreated with the right-wing faction, and maybe even gone into emigration, than have to work for the victorious Communists. However, he was prevented from doing this as just at this time he became seriously ill with typhus, and so remained behind when the Whites fled. Incidentally, both his brothers had fled abroad, and were by this time living in Paris.

From 1920 to 1921 Bulgakov briefly worked in a hospital in the Caucasus, where he had been deployed by the Whites, who finally retreated from there in 1922. Bulgakov, living in the town of Vladikavkaz, produced a series of journalistic sketches, later collected and published as *Notes on Shirt Cuffs*, detailing his own experiences at the time, and later in Moscow. He avowedly took as his model classic writers such as Molière, Gogol and particularly Pushkin, and his writings at this time attracted criticism from anti-White critics, because of what was seen as his old-fashioned style and material, which was still that of the cultured European intellectuals of an earlier age, rather than being in keeping with the fresh aspirations of the new progressive proletarian era inaugurated by the Communists. The authorities championed literature and works of art which depicted the life of the masses and assisted in the development of the new Communist ethos. At the time, this tendency was still only on the level of advice and encouragement from the Government, rather than being a categorical demand. It only began to crystallize around the mid-1920s into an obligatory uncompromising line, ultimately leading to the repression, under Stalin, of any kind of even mildly dissident work, and to an increasingly oppressive state surveillance.

In fact, although never a supporter of Bolshevism as such, Bulgakov's articles of the early 1920s display not approval of the Red rule, but simply relief that at last there seemed to be stable government in Russia, which had re-established law and order and was gradually rebuilding the country's infrastructure. However, this relief at the new stability did not prevent him producing stories satirizing the new social order; for instance, around this time he published an experimental satirical novella entitled *Crimson Island*, purporting to be a novella by "Comrade Jules Verne" translated from the French. It portrayed the Whites as stereotypical monsters and was written in the coarse, cliché-ridden agitprop style of the time – a blatant lampoon of the genre.

But by 1921, when he was approaching the age of thirty, Bulgakov was becoming worried that he still had no solid body of work behind him. Life had always been a struggle for him and his wife Tatyana, but he had now begun to receive some money from his writing and to mix in Russian artistic circles. After his medical service in Vladikavkaz he moved to Moscow, where he earned a precarious living over the next few years, contributing sketches to newspapers and magazines, and lecturing on literature. In January 1924 he met the sophisticated, multilingual Lyubov Belozerskaya, who was the wife of a journalist. In comparison with her, Tatyana seemed provincial and uncultured. They started a relationship, divorced their respective partners, and were entered in the local registers as married in late spring 1924, though the exact date of their marriage is unclear.

Between 1925 and 1926 Bulgakov produced three anthologies of his stories, the major one of which received the overall title *Diaboliad*. This collection received reasonably favourable reviews. One compared his stories in *Diaboliad* to those of Gogol, and this was in fact the only major volume of his fiction to be published in the USSR during his lifetime. According to a typist he employed at this time, he would dictate to her for two or three hours every day, from notebooks and loose sheets of paper, though not apparently from any completely composed manuscript.

But in a review in the newspaper *Izvestiya* of *Diaboliad* and some of Bulgakov's other writings in September 1925, the Marxist writer and critic Lev Averbakh, who was to become head of RAPP (the Russian Association of Proletarian Writers) had already declared that the stories contained only one theme: the uselessness and chaos arising from the Communists' attempts to create a new society. The critic then warned that, although Soviet satire was permissible and indeed requisite for the purposes of stimulating the restructuring of society, totally destructive lampoons such as Bulgakov's were irrelevant, and even inimical to the new ethos.

The Government's newly established body for overseeing literature subsequently ordered *Diaboliad* to be withdrawn, although it allowed a reissue in early 1926. By April 1925, Bulgakov was reading his long story *A Dog's Heart* at literary gatherings, but finding it very difficult to get this work, or anything else, published. In May 1926, Bulgakov's flat was searched by agents of OGPU, the precursor of the KGB. The typescript of *A Dog's Heart* and Bulgakov's most recent diaries were confiscated; the story was only published in full in Russian in 1968 (in Germany), and in the USSR only in 1987, in a literary journal. In 1926

Bulgakov had written a stage adaptation of the story, but again it was only produced for the first time in June 1987, after which it became extremely popular throughout the USSR.

The White Guard   Between 1922 and 1924 Bulgakov was engaged in writing his first novel, ultimately to be known as *The White Guard*. The publishing history of this volume – which was originally planned to be the first part of a trilogy portraying the whole sweep of the Russian Revolution and Civil War – is extremely complex, and there were several different redactions. The whole project was very important to him, and was written at a period of great material hardship. By 1925 he was reading large sections at literary gatherings. Most of the chapters were published as they were produced, in literary magazines, with the exception of the ending, which was banned by the censors; pirated editions, with concocted endings, were published abroad. The novel appeared finally, substantially rewritten and complete, in 1929 in Paris, in a version approved by the author. Contrary to all other Soviet publications of this period, which saw the events of these years from the point of view of the victorious Bolsheviks, Bulgakov described that time from the perspective of one of the enemy factions, portraying them not as vile and sadistic monsters, as was now the custom, but as ordinary human beings with their own problems, fears and ideals.

It had a mixed reception; one review found it inferior to his short stories, while another compared it to the novelistic debut of Dostoevsky. It made almost no stir, and it's interesting to note that, in spite of the fact that the atmosphere was becoming more and more repressive as to the kind of artistic works which would be permitted, the party newspaper *Pravda* in 1927 could write neutrally of its "interesting point of view from a White-Guard perspective".

First Plays   Representatives of the Moscow Arts Theatre (MAT) had heard Bulgakov reading extracts from his novel-in-progress at literary events, realized its dramatic potential, and asked him to adapt the novel for the stage. The possibility had dawned on him even before this, and it seems he was making drafts for such a play from early 1925. This play – now known as *The Days of the Turbins* – had an extremely complicated history. At rehearsals, Bulgakov was interrogated by OGPU. MAT forwarded the original final version to Anatoly Lunacharsky, the People's Commissar for Education, to verify whether it was sufficiently innocuous politically for them to be able to stage it. He wrote back declaring it was rubbish from an artistic point of view, but as far as subject matter went there was no problem. The theatre seems to have agreed with him as to the literary merit of the piece, since they encouraged the author to embark on an extensive revision, which would ultimately produce a radically different version.

During rehearsals as late as August 1926, representatives of OGPU and the censors were coming to the theatre to hold lengthy negotiations with the author and director, and to suggest alterations. The play was finally passed for performance, but only at MAT – no productions were to be permitted anywhere else. It was only allowed to be staged elsewhere, oddly enough, from 1933 onwards, when the party line was being enforced more and more rigorously and Stalin's reign was becoming increasingly repressive. Rumour had it that Stalin himself had quite enjoyed the play when he saw it at MAT in 1929, regarded its contents as innocuous, and had himself authorized its wider performances.

It was ultimately premiered on 26th October 1926, and achieved great acclaim, becoming known as "the second *Seagull*", as the first performance of Chekhov's *Seagull* at MAT in 1898 had inaugurated the theatre's financial and artistic success after a long period of mediocrity and falling popularity. This was a turning point in the fortunes of MAT, which had been coming under fire for only performing the classics and not adopting styles of acting and subject matter more in keeping with modern times and themes. The play was directed by one of the original founders of MAT, Konstantin Stanislavsky, and he authorized a thousand-rouble advance for the playwright, which alleviated somewhat the severe financial constraints he had been living under.

The play received mixed reviews, depending almost entirely on the journal or reviewer's political views. One critic objected to its "idealization of the Bolsheviks' enemies", while another vilified its "petit-bourgeois vulgarity". Others accused it of using means of expression dating from the era of classic theatre which had now been replaced in contemporary plays by styles – often crudely propagandistic – which were more in tune with the Soviet proletarian ethos. The piece was extremely popular, however, and in spite of the fact that it was only on in one theatre, Bulgakov could live reasonably well on his share of the royalties.

171

At this time another Moscow theatre, the Vakhtangov, also requested a play from the author, so Bulgakov gave them *Zoyka's Apartment*, which had probably been written in late 1925. It was premiered on 28th October, just two days after *The Days of the Turbins*. The theatre's representatives suggested a few textual (not political) changes, and Bulgakov first reacted with some irritation, then acknowledged he had been overworked and under stress, due to the strain of the negotiations with OGPU and the censors over *The Days of the Turbins*.

Various other changes had to be made before the censors were satisfied, but the play was allowed to go on tour throughout the Soviet Union. It is rather surprising that it was permitted, because, in line with party doctrine, social and sexual mores were beginning to become more and more puritanical, and the play brought out into the open the seamier side of life which still existed in the workers' paradise. Zoyka's apartment is in fact a high-class brothel, and the Moscow papers had recently reported the discovery in the city of various such establishments, as well as drug dens. The acting and production received rave reviews, but the subject matter was condemned by some reviewers as philistine and shallow, and the appearance of scantily clad actresses on stage was excoriated as being immoral.

The play was extremely successful, both in Moscow and on tour, and brought the author further substantial royalties. Bulgakov was at this time photographed wearing a monocle and looking extremely dandified; those close to him claimed that the monocle was worn for genuine medical reasons, but this photograph attracted personal criticism in the press: he was accused of living in the past and being reactionary.

Perhaps to counteract this out-of-touch image, Bulgakov published a number of sketches in various journals between 1925 and 1927 giving his reminiscences of medical practice in the remote countryside. When finally collected and published posthumously, they were given the title *A Young Doctor's Notebook*. Although they were written principally to alleviate his financial straits, the writer may also have been trying to demonstrate that, in spite of all the criticism, he was a useful member of society with his medical knowledge.

Censorship   Bulgakov's next major work was the play *Escape* (also translated as *Flight*), which, according to dates on some of the manuscript pages, was written and revised between 1926 and 1928. The script was thoroughly rewritten in 1932 and only performed in the USSR in 1957. The play was banned at the rehearsal stage in 1929 as being not sufficiently "revolutionary", though Bulgakov claimed in bafflement that he had in fact been trying to write a piece that was more akin to agitprop than anything he'd previously written.

Escape is set in the Crimea during the struggle between the Whites and Reds in the Civil War, and portrays the Whites as stereotypical villains involved in prostitution, corruption and terror. At first it seems perplexing that the piece should have been banned, since it seems so in tune with the spirit of the times, but given Bulgakov's well-known old-fashioned and anti-Red stance, the play may well have been viewed as in fact a satire on the crude agitprop pieces of the time.

The year 1929 was cataclysmic both for Bulgakov and for other Soviet writers: by order of RAPP (Russian Association of Proletarian Writers) *Escape*, *The Days of the Turbins* and *Zoyka's Apartment* had their productions suspended. Although, with the exception of *Zoyka*, they were then granted temporary runs, at least until the end of that season, their long-term future remained uncertain.

Bulgakov had apparently started drafting his masterpiece *The Master and Margarita* as early as 1928. The novel had gone through at least six revisions by the time of the writer's death in 1940. With the tightening of the party line, there was an increase in militant, politically approved atheism, and one of the novel's major themes is a retelling of Christ's final days, and his victory in defeat – possibly a response to the atheism of Bulgakov's time. He submitted one chapter, under a pseudonym, to the magazine *Nedra* in May 1929, which described satirically the intrigues among the official literary bodies of the time, such as RAPP and others. This chapter was rejected. Yevgeny Zamyatin, another writer in disfavour at the time, who finally emigrated permanently, stated privately that the Soviet Government was adopting the worst excesses of old Spanish Catholicism, seeing heresies where there were none.

In July of that year Bulgakov wrote a letter to Stalin and other leading politicians and writers in good standing with the authorities, asking to be allowed to leave the USSR with his wife; he stated in this letter that it appeared he would never be allowed to be published or performed again in his own country. His next play, *Molière*, was about problems faced by the French playwright in the period of the autocratic monarch Louis XIV; the parallels between the times of Molière and the Soviet writer are blatant. It was read in January 1930 to the Artistic Board of MAT, who reported that, although it had "no relevance to contemporary questions", they had now admitted a couple of modern propaganda plays to their repertoire, and so they thought the authorities might stretch a point and permit Bulgakov's play. But in March he was told that the Government artistic authorities had not passed the piece. MAT now demanded the return of the thousand-rouble advance they had allowed Bulgakov for *Escape*, also now banned; furthermore the writer was plagued by demands for unpaid income tax relating to the previous year. None of his works were now in production.

Help from Stalin   On Good Friday Bulgakov received a telephone call from Stalin himself promising a favourable response to his letter to the authorities, either to be allowed to emigrate, or at least to be permitted to take up gainful employment in a theatre if he so wished. Stalin even promised a personal meeting with the writer. Neither meeting nor response ever materialized, but Bulgakov was shortly afterwards appointed Assistant Director at MAT, and Consultant to the Theatre of Working Youth, probably as a result of some strings being pulled in high places. Although unsatisfactory, these officially sanctioned positions provided the writer with some income and measure of protection against the torrent of arbitrary arrests now sweeping through the country.

Yelena   Although there was now some stability in Bulgakov's profes-
Shilovskaya   sional life, there was to be another major turn in his love life. In February 1929 he had met at a friend's house in Moscow a woman called Yelena Shilovskaya; she was married with two children, highly cultured, and was personal secretary at MAT to the world-famous theatre director Vladimir Nemirovich-Danchenko. They fell in love, but then did not see each other again for around eighteen months. When they did meet again, they found they were still drawn to each other, divorced their partners, and married in October 1932. She remained his wife till his death, and afterwards became the keeper of his archives and worked tirelessly to have his works published.

Over the next few years Bulgakov wrote at least twice more to Stalin asking to be allowed to emigrate. But permission was not forthcoming, and so Bulgakov would never travel outside the USSR. He always felt deprived because of this and sensed something had been lacking in his education. At this time, because of his experience in writing such letters, and because of his apparent "pull" in high places, other intellectuals such as Stanislavsky and Anna Akhmatova were asking for his help in writing similar letters.

While working at MAT, Bulgakov's enthusiasm quickly waned and he felt creatively stifled as his adaptations for the stage of such classic Russian novels as Gogol's *Dead Souls* were altered extensively either for political or artistic reasons. However, despite these changes, he also provided screenplays for mooted films of both *Dead Souls* and Gogol's play *The Government Inspector*. Once again, neither ever came to fruition. There were further projects at this time for other major theatres, both in Moscow and Leningrad, such as an adaptation of Tolstoy's novel *War and Peace* for the stage. This too never came to anything. In May 1932 he wrote: "In nine days' time I shall be celebrating my forty-first birthday... And so towards the conclusion of my literary career I've been forced to write adaptations. A brilliant finale, don't you think?" He wrote numerous other plays and adaptations between then and the end of his life, but no new works were ever produced on stage.

Things appeared to be looking up at one point, because in October 1931 *Molière* had been passed by the censors for production and was accepted by the Bolshoi Drama Theatre in Leningrad. Moreover, in 1932, MAT had made a routine request to be allowed to restage certain works, and to their surprise were permitted to put *Zoyka's Apartment* and *The Days of the Turbins* back into their schedules. This initially seemed to herald a new thaw, a new liberalism, and these prospects were enhanced by the dissolution of such bodies as RAPP, and the formation of the Soviet Writers' Union. Writers hitherto regarded with suspicion were published.

However, although *Molière* was now in production at the Leningrad theatre, the theatre authorities withdrew it suddenly, terrified by the vituperative attacks of a revolutionary and hard-line Communist playwright, Vsevolod Vishnevsky, whose works celebrated the heroic deeds of the Soviet armed forces and working people and who would place a gun on the table when reading a play aloud.

Bulgakov was then commissioned to write a biography of Molière for the popular market, and the typescript was submitted to the authorities in March 1933. However, it was once again rejected, because Bulgakov, never one to compromise,

175

had adopted an unorthodox means of telling his story, having a flamboyant narrator within the story laying out the known details of Molière's life, but also commenting on them and on the times in which he lived; parallels with modern Soviet times were not hard to find. The censor who rejected Bulgakov's work suggested the project should only be undertaken by a "serious Soviet historian". It was finally published only in 1962, and was one of the writer's first works to be issued posthumously. It is now regarded as a major work, both in content and style.

Acting   In December 1934 Bulgakov made his acting debut for MAT as the judge in an adaptation of Dickens's *Pickwick Papers*, and the performance was universally described as hilarious and brilliant. However, though he obviously had great acting ability, he found the stress and the commitment of performing night after night a distraction from his career as a creative writer. He was still attempting to write plays and other works – such as *Ivan Vasilyevich*, set in the time of Ivan the Terrible – which were rejected by the authorities.

At about this time, Bulgakov proposed a play on the life of Alexander Pushkin, and both Shostakovich and Prokofiev expressed an interest in turning the play into an opera. But then Shostakovich's opera *Lady Macbeth of Mtsensk* was slaughtered in the press for being ideologically and artistically unsound, and Bulgakov's play, which had not even gone into production, was banned in January 1936.

Molière, in a revised form, was passed for performance in late 1935, and premiered by MAT in February 1936. However, it was promptly savaged by the newspaper *Pravda* for its "falsity", and MAT immediately withdrew it from the repertoire. Bulgakov, bitterly resentful at the theatre's abject capitulation, resigned later in the year, and swiftly joined the famous Moscow Bolshoi Opera Theatre as librettist and adviser. In November 1936, in just a few hours he churned out *Black Snow* (later to be called *A Theatrical Novel*), a short satire on the recent events at MAT.

Play on Stalin   In mid-1937 he began intensive work on yet another redaction of *The Master and Margarita*, which was finally typed out by June 1938. Soon afterwards, he started work on a play about Stalin, *Batum*. The dictator, although in the main disapproving of the tendency of Bulgakov's works, still found them interesting, and had always extended a certain amount of protection to him. Bulgakov had started work in 1936 on a history of the USSR for schools and, although the project remained fragmentary, he had gathered a tremendous amount of material on Stalin for the project, which he proposed to incorporate in his play. It is odd that this ruthless dictator and Bulgakov – who was certainly not a supporter of the regime and whose patrician views seemed to date from a previous era – should have been locked in such a relationship of mutual fascination.

Although MAT told him that the play on Stalin would do both him and the theatre good in official eyes, Bulgakov, still contemptuous of the theatre, demanded that they provide him with a new flat where he could work without interruption from noise. MAT complied with this condition. He submitted the manuscript in July 1939, but it was turned down, apparently by the dictator himself.

Bulgakov was devastated by this rejection, and almost immediately began to suffer a massive deterioration in health. His eyesight became worse and worse, he developed appalling headaches, he grew extremely sensitive to light and often could not leave his flat for days on end. All this was the first manifestation of the sclerosis of the kidneys which finally killed him, as it had killed his father. When he could, he continued revising *The Master and Margarita*, but only managed to finish correcting the first part. He became totally bedridden, his weight fell to under fifty kilograms, and he finally died on 10th March 1940. The next morning a call came through from Stalin's office – though not from the leader himself – asking whether it was true the writer was dead. On receiving the answer, the caller hung up with no comment. Bulgakov had had no new work published or performed for some time, yet the Soviet Writers' Union, full of many of the people who had pilloried him so mercilessly over the years, honoured him respectfully. He was buried in the Novodevichy Cemetery, in the section for artistic figures, near Chekhov and Gogol. Ultimately, a large stone which had lain on Gogol's grave, but had been replaced by a memorial bust, was placed on Bulgakov's grave, where it still lies.

Illness and Death

After the Second World War ended in 1945, the country had other priorities than the publication of hitherto banned authors, but Bulgakov's wife campaigned fearlessly for his rehabilitation, and in 1957 *The Days of the Turbins* and his play on the end of Pushkin's life were published, and a larger selection of his plays appeared in 1962. A heavily cut version of *The Master and Margarita* appeared in a specialist

Posthumous Publications and Reputation

literary journal throughout 1966–67, and the full uncensored text in 1973. Subsequently – especially post-Glasnost – more and more works of Bulgakov's were published in uncensored redactions, and at last Western publishers could see the originals of what they had frequently published before in corrupt smuggled variants. Bulgakov's third wife maintained his archive, and both she and his second wife gave public lectures on him, wrote memoirs of him and campaigned for publication of his works. Bulgakov has now achieved cult status in Russia, and almost all of his works have been published in uncensored editions, with unbiased editorial commentary and annotation.

Mikhail Bulgakov's Works

It is difficult to give an overall survey of Bulgakov's works, which, counting short stories and adaptations, approach a total of almost one hundred. Many of these works exist in several versions, as the author revised them constantly to make them more acceptable to the authorities. This meant that published versions – including translations brought out abroad – were frequently not based on what the author might have considered the "definitive" version. In fact to talk of "definitive versions" with reference to Bulgakov's works may be misleading. Furthermore, no new works of his were published after 1927, and they only began to be issued sporadically, frequently in censored versions, from 1962 onwards. Complete and uncut editions of many of the works have begun to appear only from the mid-1990s. Therefore the section below will contain only the most prominent works in all genres.

Themes   Despite the wide variety of settings of his novels – Russia, the Caucasus, Ukraine, Jerusalem in New Testament times and the Paris of Louis XIV – the underlying themes of Bulgakov's works remain remarkably constant throughout his career. Although these works contain a huge number of characters, most of them conform to certain archetypes and patterns of behaviour.

Stylistically, Bulgakov was influenced by early-nineteenth-century classic Russian writers such as Gogol and Pushkin, and he espoused the values of late-nineteenth-century liberal democracy and culture, underpinned by Christian teachings. Although Bulgakov came from an ecclesiastical background, he was never in fact a conventional believer, but, like many agnostic or atheistic Russian nineteenth-century intellectuals and artists, he respected the role that the basic teachings of religion had played in forming Russian and European culture – although they, and Bulgakov, had no liking for the way religions upheld obscurantism and authority.

Some works portray the struggle of the outsider against society, such as the play and narrative based on the life of Molière, or the novel *The Master and Margarita*, in which the outsider persecuted by society and the state is Yeshua, i.e. Jesus. Other works give prominent roles to doctors and scientists, and demonstrate what happens if science is misused and is subjected to Government interference. Those works portraying historical reality, such as *The White Guard*, show the Whites – who were normally depicted in Communist literature as evil reactionaries – to be ordinary human beings with their own concerns and ideals. Most of all, Bulgakov's work is pervaded by a biting satire on life as he saw it around him in the USSR, especially in the artistic world, and there is frequently a "magical realist" element – as in *The Master and Margarita* – in which contemporary reality and fantasy are intermingled, or which show the influence of Western science fiction (Bulgakov admired the works of H.G. Wells enormously).

Bulgakov's major works are written in a variety of forms, *The White Guard* including novels, plays and short stories. His first novel, *The White Guard*, was written between 1922 and 1924, but it received numerous substantial revisions later. It was originally conceived as the first volume of a trilogy portraying the entire sweep of the post-revolutionary Civil War from a number of different points of view. Although this first and only volume was criticized for showing events from the viewpoint of the Whites, the third volume would apparently have given the perspective of the Communists. Many chapters of the novel were published separately in literary journals as they appeared. The ending – the dreams presaging disaster for the country – never appeared, because the journal it was due to be printed in, *Rossiya*, was shut down by official order, precisely because it was publishing such material as Bulgakov's. Different pirate versions, with radically variant texts and concocted endings, appeared abroad. The novel only appeared complete in Russian, having been proofread by the author, in 1929 in Paris, where there was a substantial émigré population from the Tsarist Empire/USSR.

The major part of the story takes place during the forty-seven days in which the Ukrainian Nationalists, under their leader

Petlyura, held power in Kiev. The novel ends in February 1919, when Petlyura was overthrown by the Bolsheviks. The major protagonists are the Turbins, a family reminiscent of Bulgakov's own, with a similar address, who also work in the medical profession: many elements of the novel are in fact autobiographical. At the beginning of the novel, we are still in the world of old Russia, with artistic and elegant furniture dating from the Tsarist era, and a piano, books and high-quality pictures on the walls. But the atmosphere is one of fear about the future, and apprehension at the world collapsing. The Turbins' warm flat, in which the closely knit family can take refuge from the events outside, is progressively encroached on by reality. Nikolka Turbin, the younger son, is still at high school and in the cadet corps; he has a vague feeling that he should be fighting on the side of the Whites – that is, the forces who were against both the Nationalists and Communists. However, when a self-sacrificing White soldier dies in the street in Nikolka's arms, he realizes for the first time that war is vile. Near the conclusion of the novel there is a family gathering at the flat, but everything has changed since the beginning of the book: relationships have been severed, and there is no longer any confidence in the future. As the Ukrainian Nationalists flee, they brutally murder a Jew near the Turbins' flat, demonstrating that liberal tolerant values have disintegrated. The novel ends with a series of sinister apocalyptic dreams – indeed the novel contains imagery throughout from the Biblical Apocalypse. These dreams mainly presage catastrophe for the family and society, although the novel ends with the very short dream of a child, which does seem to prefigure some sort of peace in the distant future.

The Life of Monsieur de Molière   *The Life of Monsieur de Molière* is sometimes classed not as a novel but as a biography. However, the treatment is distinctive enough to enable the work to be ranked as semi-fictionalized. Bulgakov's interpretative view of the French writer's life, rather than a purely historical perspective, is very similar to that in his play on the same theme. The book was written in 1932, but was banned for the same reasons which were to cause problems later for the play. Molière's life is narrated in the novel by an intermediary, a flamboyant figure who often digresses, and frequently comments on the political intrigues of the French author's time. The censors may have felt that the description of the French writer's relationship to an autocrat might have borne too many similarities to Bulgakov's relationship to Stalin.

The book was only finally published in the USSR in 1962, and is now regarded as a major work.

Although he had written fragmentary pieces about the theatre before, Bulgakov only really settled down to produce a longer work on the theme – a short, vicious satire on events in the Soviet theatre – in November 1936, after what he saw as MAT's abject capitulation in the face of attacks by Communists on *Molière*. *A Theatrical Novel* was only published for the first time in the Soviet Union in 1969. There is a short introduction, purporting to be by an author who has found a manuscript written by a theatrical personage who has committed suicide (the reason for Bulgakov's original title, *Notes of the Deceased*; other mooted titles were *Black Snow* and *White Snow*). Not only does Bulgakov take a swipe at censorship and the abject and pusillanimous authorities of the theatre world, but he also deals savagely with the reputations of such people as the theatre director Stanislavsky, who, despite his fame abroad, is depicted – in a thinly veiled portrait – as a tyrannical figure who crushes the individuality and flair of writers and actors in the plays which he is directing. The manuscript ends inconclusively, with the dead writer still proclaiming his wonder at the nature of theatre itself, despite its intrigues and frustrations; the original author who has found the manuscript does not reappear, and it's uncertain whether the point is that the theatrical figure left his memoirs uncompleted, or whether in fact Bulgakov failed to finish his original project.

The Master and Margarita is generally regarded as Bulgakov's masterpiece. He worked on it from 1928 to 1940, and it exists in at least six different variants, ranging from the fragmentary to the large-scale narrative which he was working on at the onset of the illness from which he died. Even the first redaction contains many of the final elements, although the Devil is the only narrator of the story of Pilate and Jesus – the insertion of the Master and Margarita came at a later stage. In 1929 the provisional title was *The Engineer's Hoof* (the word "engineer" had become part of the vocabulary of the Soviet demonology of the times, since in May and June 1928 a large group of mining engineers had been tried for anti-revolutionary activities, and they were equated in the press to the Devil who was trying to undermine the new Soviet society). The last variant written before the author's death was completed around mid-1938, and Bulgakov began proofreading and revising it, making numerous

A Theatrical Novel

The Master and Margarita

181

corrections and sorting out loose ends. In his sick state, he managed to revise only the first part of the novel, and there are still a certain number of moot points remaining later on. The novel was first published in a severely cut version in 1966–67, in a specialist Russian literary journal, while the complete text was published only in 1973. At one stage, Bulgakov apparently intended to allow Stalin to be the first reader of *The Master and Margarita*, and to present him with a personal copy.

The multi-layered narrative switches backwards and forwards between Jerusalem in the time of Christ and contemporary Moscow. The Devil – who assumes the name Woland – visits Moscow with his entourage, which includes a large talking black cat and a naked witch, and they cause havoc with their displays of magic.

In the scenes set in modern times, the narrative indirectly evokes the atmosphere of a dictatorship. This is paralleled in the Pilate narrative by the figure of Caesar, who, although he is mentioned, never appears.

The atheists of modern Moscow who, following the contemporary party line, snigger at Christ's miracles and deny his existence, are forced to create explanations for what they see the Devil doing in front of them in their own city.

There are numerous references to literature, and also to music – there are three characters with the names of composers, Berlioz, Stravinsky and Rimsky-Korsakov. Berlioz the composer wrote an oratorio on the theme of Faust, who is in love with the self-sacrificing Margarita; immediately we are drawn towards the idea that the persecuted writer known as the Master, who also has a devoted lover called Margarita, is a modern manifestation of Faust. Bulgakov carried out immense research on studies of ancient Jerusalem and theology, particularly Christology. The novel demands several readings, such are the depths of interconnected details and implications.

Days of the Turbins   Apart from novels, another important area for Bulgakov to channel his creative energy into was plays. *The Days of the Turbins* was the first of his works to be staged: it was commissioned by the Moscow Arts Theatre in early 1925, although it seems Bulgakov had already thought of the possibility of a stage adaptation of *The White Guard*, since acquaintances report him making drafts for such a project slightly earlier. It had an extremely complex history, which involved numerous rewritings after constant negotiations between the writer, theatre, secret police and censors. Bulgakov did not want to leave any elements of the novel out, but on his reading the initial manuscript at the Moscow Arts Theatre it was found to be far too long, and so he cut out a few of the minor characters and pruned the dream sequences in the novel. However, the background is still the same – the Civil War in Kiev after the Bolshevik Revolution. The family are broadly moderate Tsarists in their views, and therefore are anti-Communist but, being ethnically Russian, have no sympathy with the Ukrainian Nationalists either, and so end up fighting for the White Guards. Their flat at the beginning is almost Chekhovian in its warmth, cosiness and air of old-world culture, but by the end one brother has been killed in the fighting and, as the sounds of the 'Internationale' offstage announce the victory of the Communists, a feeling of apprehension grips the family as their world seems to be collapsing round them. The final lines of the play communicate these misgivings (Nikolka: "Gentlemen, this evening is a great prologue to a new historical play." / Studzinsky: "For some a prologue – for others an epilogue."). The final sentence may be taken as representing Bulgakov's fear about the effect the Communist takeover might have on the rest of his own career.

The Soviet playwright Viktor Nekrasov, who was in favour of the Revolution, commented that the play was an excellent recreation of that time in Kiev, where he had also been participating in the historic events on the Bolshevik side – the atmosphere was all very familiar, Nekrasov confirmed, and one couldn't help extending sympathy to such characters as the Turbins, even if they were on the other side: they were simply individuals caught up in historical events.

At around the time of the writing of *The Days of the Turbins*, another Moscow theatre, the Vakhtangov, requested a play from Bulgakov, so he provided them with *Zoyka's Apartment*, which had been first drafted in late 1925. Various alterations had to be made before the censors were satisfied. At least four different texts of *Zoyka* exist, the final revision completed as late as 1935; this last is now regarded as the authoritative text, and is that generally translated for Western editions.

The setting is a Moscow apartment run by Zoyka; it operates as a women's dress shop and haute-couturier during the

Zoyka's Apartment

day, and becomes a brothel after closing time. At the time the play was written, various brothels and drug dens had been unearthed by the police in the capital, some run by Chinese nationals. Bulgakov's play contains therefore not only easily recognizable political and social types who turn up for a session with the scantily clad ladies, but also stereotypical Chinese drug dealers and addicts. Zoyka is however treated with moral neutrality by the author: she operates as the madam of the brothel in order to raise money as fast as possible so that she can emigrate abroad with her husband, an impoverished former aristocrat, who is also a drug addict. In the final act the ladies and clients dance to decadent Western popular music, a fight breaks out and a man is murdered. The play ends with the establishment being raided by "unknown strangers", who are presumably government inspectors and the police. At this point the final curtain comes down, so we never find out the ultimate fate of the characters.

The Crimson Island   In 1924 Bulgakov had written a rather unsubtle short story, *The Crimson Island*, which was a parody of the crude agitprop style of much of the literature of the time, with its stereotypical heroic and noble Communists, and evil reactionaries and foreigners trying to undermine the new Communist state, all written in the language of the person in the street – often as imagined by educated people who had no direct knowledge of this working-class language. In 1927 he adapted this parody for the stage. The play bears the subtitle: *The Dress Rehearsal of a Play by Citizen Jules Verne in Gennady Panfilovich's theatre, with music, a volcanic eruption and English sailors: in four acts, with a prologue and an epilogue.* The play was much more successful than the story. He offered it to the Kamerny ["Chamber"] Theatre, in Moscow, which specialized in mannered and elegant productions, still in the style of the late 1890s; it was passed for performance and premiered in December 1928, and was a success, though some of the more left-wing of the audience and critics found it hard to swallow. However, the critic Novitsky wrote that it was an "interesting and witty parody, satirizing what crushes artistic creativity and cultivates slavish and absurd dramatic characters, removing the individuality from actors and writers and creating idols, lickspittles and panegyrists". The director of the play, Alexander Tairov, claimed that the work was meant to be self-criticism of the falsity and crudeness of some revolutionary work. Most reviews found it amusing and harmless, and it attracted good audiences. However, there were just a few vitriolic reviews; Stalin himself commented that the production of such a play underlined how reactionary the Kamerny Theatre still was. The work was subsequently banned by the censor in March 1929.

The Crimson Island takes the form of a play within a play: the prologue and epilogue take place in the theatre where the play is to be rehearsed and performed; the playwright – who, although Russian, has taken the pen name Jules Verne – is progressive and sensitive, but his original work is increasingly censored and altered out of all recognition. The rest of the acts show the rewritten play, which has now become a crude agitprop piece. The play within *Crimson Island* takes place on a sparsely populated desert island run by a white king and ruling class, with black underlings. There is a volcano rumbling in the background, which occasionally erupts. The wicked foreigners are represented by the English Lord and Lady Aberaven, who sail in on a yacht crewed by English sailors who march on singing 'It's a Long Way to Tipperary'. During the play the island's underlings stage a revolution and try unsuccessfully to urge the English sailors to rebel against the evil Lord and Lady. However, they do not succeed, and the wicked aristocrats sail away unharmed, leaving the revolutionaries in control of the island.

Bulgakov's play *Escape* (also translated as *Flight*), drafted between 1926 and 1928, and completely rewritten in 1932, is set in the Crimea during the conflicts between the Whites and Reds in the Civil War after the Revolution. *Escape*

The Whites – who include a general who has murdered people in cold blood – emigrate to Constantinople, but find they are not accepted by the locals, and their living conditions are appalling. One of the women has to support them all by resorting to prostitution. The murderous White general nurses his colleagues during an outbreak of typhus, and feels he has expiated some of his guilt for the crimes he has committed against humanity. He and a few of his colleagues decide to return to the USSR, since even life under Communism cannot be as bad as in Turkey. However, the censors objected that these people were coming back for negative reasons – simply to get away from where they were – and not because they had genuinely come to believe in the Revolution, or had the welfare of the working people at heart.

Molière   Molière was one of Bulgakov's favourite writers, and some aspects of his writing seemed relevant to Soviet reality – for example the character of the fawning, scheming, hypocritical anti-hero of *Tartuffe*. Bulgakov's next play, *Molière*, was about problems faced by the French playwright during the reign of the autocratic monarch Louis XIV. It was written between October and December 1929 and, as seen above, submitted in January 1930 to the Artistic Board of MAT. Bulgakov told them that he had not written an overtly political piece, but one about a writer hounded by a cabal of critics in connivance with the absolute monarch. Unfortunately, despite MAT's optimism, the authorities did not permit a production. In this piece the French writer at one stage, like Bulgakov, intends to leave the country permanently. Late in the play, the King realizes that Molière's brilliance would be a further ornament to his resplendent court, and extends him his protection; however, then this official attitude changes, Molière is once again an outcast, and he dies on stage, while acting in one of his own plays, a broken man. The play's original title was *The Cabal of Hypocrites*, but it was probably decided that this was too contentious.

Bliss   A version of the play *Bliss* appears to have been drafted in
and   1929, but was destroyed and thoroughly rewritten between then
Ivan Vasilyevich   and 1934. Bulgakov managed to interest both the Leningrad Music Hall Theatre and Moscow Satire Theatre in the idea, but they both said it would be impossible to stage because of the political climate of the time, and told him to rewrite it; accordingly he transferred the original plot to the time of Tsar Ivan the Terrible in the sixteenth century, and the new play, entitled *Ivan Vasilyevich*, was completed by late 1935.

The basic premise behind both plays is the same: an inventor builds a time machine (as mentioned above, Bulgakov was a great admirer of H.G. Wells) and travels to a very different period of history: present-day society is contrasted starkly with the world he has travelled to. However, in *Bliss*, the contrasted world is far in the future, while in *Ivan Vasilyevich* it is almost four hundred years in the past. In *Bliss* the inventor accidentally takes a petty criminal and a typically idiotic building manager from his own time to the Moscow of 2222: it is a utopian society, with no police and no denunciations to the authorities. He finally returns to his own time with the criminal and the building manager, but also with somebody from the future who is fed up with the bland and boring conformity of such a paradise

(Bulgakov was always sceptical of the idea of any utopia, not just the Communist one).

Ivan Vasilyevich is set in the Moscow of the tyrannical Tsar, and therefore the contrast between a paradise and present reality is not the major theme. In fact, contemporary Russian society is almost presented favourably in contrast with the distant past. However, when the inventor and his crew – including a character from Ivan's time who has been transported to the present accidentally – arrive back in modern Moscow, they are all promptly arrested and the play finishes, emphasizing that, although modern times are an improvement on the distant past, the problems of that remote period still exist in contemporary reality. For all the differences in period and emphasis, most of the characters of the two plays are the same, and have very similar speeches.

Even this watered-down version of the original theme was rejected by the theatres it was offered to, who thought that it would still be unperformable. It was only premiered in the Soviet Union in 1966. Bulgakov tried neutering the theme even further, most notably by tacking on an ending in which the inventor wakes up in his Moscow flat with the music of Rimsky-Korsakov's popular opera *The Maid of Pskov* (set in Ivan the Terrible's time) wafting in from offstage, presumably meant to be from a radio in another room. The inventor gives the impression that the events of the play in Ivan's time have all been a dream brought on by the music. But all this rewriting was to no avail, and the play was never accepted by any theatre during Bulgakov's lifetime.

In January 1931 Bulgakov signed a contract with the Leningrad Red Theatre to write a play about a "future world"; he also offered it, in case of rejection, to the Vakhtangov Theatre, which had premiered *Zoyka's Apartment*. However, it was banned even before rehearsals by a visiting official from the censor's department, because it showed a cataclysmic world war in which Leningrad was destroyed. Bulgakov had seen the horror of war, including gas attacks, in his medical service, and the underlying idea of *Adam and Eve* appears to be that all war is wrong, even when waged by Communists and patriots. *Adam and Eve*

The play opens just before a world war breaks out; a poison gas is released which kills almost everybody on all sides. A scientist from the Communist camp develops an antidote, and wishes it to be available to everybody, but a patriot and a party official want it only to be distributed to people from their homeland. The Adam of the title is a cardboard caricature of a well-meaning but misguided Communist; his wife, Eve, is much less of a caricature, and is in love with the scientist who has invented the antidote. After the carnage, a world government is set up, which is neither left- nor right-wing. The scientist and Eve try to escape together, apparently to set up civilization again as the new Adam and Eve, but the sinister last line addressed to them both is: "Go, the Secretary General wants to see you." The Secretary General of the Communist Party in Russia at the time was of course Stalin, and the message may well be that even such an apparently apolitical government as that now ruling the world, which is supposed to rebuild the human race almost from nothing, is still being headed by a dictatorial character, and that the proposed regeneration of humanity has gone wrong once again from the outset and will never succeed.

The Last Days   In October 1934 Bulgakov decided to write a play about Pushkin, the great Russian poet, to be ready for the centenary of his death in 1937. He revised the original manuscript several times, but submitted it finally to the censors in late 1935. It was passed for performance, and might have been produced, but just at this time Bulgakov was in such disfavour that MAT themselves backtracked on the project.

Bulgakov, as usual, took an unusual slant on the theme: Pushkin was never to appear on stage during the piece, unless one counts the appearance at the end, in the distance, of his body being carried across stage after he has been killed in a duel. Bulgakov believed that even a great actor could not embody the full magnificence of Pushkin's achievement, the beauty of his language and his towering presence in Russian literature, let alone any of the second-rate hams who might vulgarize his image in provincial theatres. He embarked on the project at first with a Pushkin scholar, Vikenty Veresayev. However, Veresayev wanted everything written strictly in accordance with historical fact, whereas Bulgakov viewed the project dramatically. He introduced a few fictitious minor characters, and invented speeches between other characters where there is no record of what was actually said. Many events in Pushkin's life remain unclear, including who precisely engineered the duel between the army officer d'Anthès and the dangerously liberal thinker Pushkin, which resulted in the writer's death: the army, the Tsar or others? Bulgakov, while studying all the sources assiduously, put his own gloss and interpretation on these unresolved issues. In the end, Veresayev withdrew from the project in protest. The play was viewed with disfavour by critics and censors, because it implied that it may well have been the autocratic Tsar Nicholas I who was behind the events leading up to the duel, and comparison with another autocrat of modern times who also concocted plots against dissidents would inevitably have arisen in people's minds.

The Last Days was first performed in war-torn Moscow in April 1943, by MAT, since the Government was at the time striving to build up Russian morale and national consciousness in the face of enemy attack and invasion, and this play devoted to a Russian literary giant was ideal, in spite of its unorthodox perspective on events.

Commissioned by MAT in 1938, *Batum* was projected as a   *Batum* play about Joseph Stalin, mainly concerning his early life in the Caucasus, which was to be ready for his sixtieth birthday on 21st December 1939. Its first title was *Pastyr* ["The Shepherd"], in reference to Stalin's early training in a seminary for the priesthood, and to his later role as leader of his national "flock". However, although most of Bulgakov's acquaintances were full of praise for the play, and it passed the censors with no objections, it was finally rejected by the dictator himself.

Divided into four acts, the play covers the period 1898–1904, following Stalin's expulsion from the Tiflis (modern Tbilisi) Seminary, where he had been training to be an Orthodox priest, because of his anti-government activity. He is then shown in the Caucasian town of Batum organizing strikes and leading huge marches of workers to demand the release of imprisoned workers, following which he is arrested and exiled to Siberia. Stalin escapes after a month and in the last two scenes resumes the revolutionary activity which finally led to the Bolshevik Revolution under Lenin. Modern scholars have expressed scepticism as to the prominent role that Soviet biographers of Stalin's time ascribed to his period in Batum and later, and Bulgakov's play, although not disapproving of the autocrat, is objective, and far from the tone of the prevailing hagiography.

Varying explanations have been proposed as to why Stalin rejected the play. Although this was probably because it portrayed the dictator as an ordinary human being, the theory has been advanced that one of the reasons Stalin was fascinated by Bulgakov's works was precisely that the writer refused to knuckle under to the prevailing ethos, and Stalin possibly wrongly interpreted the writer's play about him as an attempt to curry favour, in the manner of all the mediocrities around him.

One Western commentator termed the writing of this play a "shameful act" on Bulgakov's part; however, the author was now beginning to show signs of severe ill health, and was perhaps understandably starting at last to feel worn down both mentally and physically by his lack of success and the constant struggle to try to make any headway in his literary career, or even to earn a crust of bread. Whatever the reasons behind the final rejection of *Batum*, Bulgakov was profoundly depressed by it, and it may have hastened his death from the hereditary sclerosis of the kidneys which he suffered from.

Bulgakov also wrote numerous short stories and novellas, the most significant of which include 'Diaboliad', 'The Fatal Eggs' and *A Dog's Heart*.

Diaboliad   'Diaboliad' was first published in the journal *Nedra* in 1924, and then reappeared as the lead story of a collection of stories under the same name in July 1925; this was in fact the last major volume brought out by the author during his lifetime in Russia, although he continued to have stories and articles published in journals for some years. In theme and treatment the story has reminiscences of Dostoevsky and Gogol.

The "hero" of the tale, a minor ordering clerk at a match factory in Moscow, misreads his boss's name – Kalsoner – as *kalsony*, i.e. "underwear". In confusion he puts through an order for underwear and is sacked. It should be mentioned here that both he and the boss have doubles, and the clerk spends the rest of the story trying to track down his boss through an increasingly nightmarish bureaucratic labyrinth, continually confusing him with his double; at the same time he is constantly having to account for misdemeanours carried out by his own double, who has a totally different personality from him, and is a raffish philanderer. The clerk is robbed of his documents and identity papers, and can no longer prove who he is – the implication being that his double is now the real him, and that he doesn't exist any longer. Finally, the petty clerk, caught up in a Kafkaesque world of bureaucracy and false appearances, goes mad and throws himself off the roof of a well-known Moscow high-rise block.

The Fatal Eggs   'The Fatal Eggs' was first published in the journal *Nedra* in early 1925, then reissued as the second story in the collection *Diaboliad*, which appeared in July 1925. The title in Russian contains a number of untranslatable puns. The major one is that a main character is named "Rokk", and the word "rok" means "fate" in Russian, so "fatal" could also mean "belonging to Rokk". Also, "eggs" is the Russian equivalent of "balls", i.e. testicles, and there is also an overtone of the "roc", i.e. the giant mythical bird in the *Thousand and One Nights*. The theme of the story is reminiscent of *The Island of Doctor Moreau* by H.G. Wells. However, Bulgakov's tale also satirizes the belief of the time, held by both scientists and journalists, that science would solve all human problems, as society moved towards utopia. Bulgakov was suspicious of such ideals and always doubted the possibility of human perfection.

In the story, a professor of zoology discovers accidentally that a certain ray will increase enormously the size of any organism or egg exposed to it – by accelerating the rate of cell multiplication – although it also increases the aggressive tendencies of any creatures contaminated in this manner. At the time, chicken plague is raging throughout Russia, all of the birds have died, and so there is a shortage of eggs. The political activist Rokk wants to get hold of the ray to irradiate eggs brought from abroad, to replenish rapidly the nation's devastated stock of poultry. The professor is reluctant, but a telephone call is received from "someone in authority" ordering him to surrender the ray. When the foreign eggs arrive at the collective farm, they look unusually large, but they are irradiated just the same. Soon Rokk's wife is devoured by an enormous snake, and the country is plagued by giant reptiles and ostriches which wreak havoc. It turns out that a batch of reptile eggs was accidentally substituted for the hens' eggs. Chaos and destruction ensue, creating a sense of panic, during which the professor is murdered. The army is mobilized unsuccessfully, but – like the providential extermination of the invaders by germs in Wells's *The War of the Worlds* – the reptiles are all wiped out by an unexpected hard summer frost. The evil ray is destroyed in a fire.

A Dog's Heart was begun in January 1925 and finished the following month. Bulgakov offered it to the journal *Nedra*, who told him it was unpublishable in the prevailing political climate; it was never issued during Bulgakov's lifetime. Its themes are reminiscent of *The Island of Doctor Moreau*, *Dr Jekyll and Mr Hyde* and *Frankenstein*.

In the tale, a doctor, Preobrazhensky ["Transfigurative", or "Transformational"] by name, transplants the pituitary glands

A Dog's Heart

191

and testicles from the corpse of a moronic petty criminal and thug into a dog (Sharik). The dog gradually takes on human form, and turns out to be a hybrid of a dog's psyche and a criminal human being. The dog's natural affectionate nature has been swamped by the viciousness of the human, who has in his turn acquired the animal appetites and instincts of the dog. The monster chooses the name Polygraf ["printing works"], and this may well have been a contemptuous reference to the numerous printing presses in Moscow churning out idiotic propaganda, appealing to the lowest common denominator in terms of intelligence and gullibility. The new creature gains employment, in keeping with his animal nature, as a cat exterminator. He is indoctrinated with party ideology by a manipulative official, and denounces numerous acquaintances to the authorities as being ideologically unsound, including his creator, the doctor. Although regarded with suspicion and warned as to his future behaviour, the doctor escapes further punishment. The hybrid creature disappears, and the dog Sharik reappears; there is a suggestion that the operation has been reversed by the doctor and his faithful assistant, and the human part of his personality has returned to its original form – a corpse – while the canine characteristics have also reassumed their natural form. Although the doctor is devastated at the evil results of his experiment, and vows to renounce all such researches in future, he appears in the last paragraph already to be delving into body parts again. The implication is that he will never be able to refrain from inventing, and the whole sorry disaster will be repeated ad infinitum. Again, as with 'The Fatal Eggs', the writer was voicing his suspicion of science and medicine's interference with nature, and his scepticism as to the possibility of utopias.

Notes on Shirt Cuffs

From 1920 to 1921, Bulgakov worked in a hospital in the Caucasus, where he produced a series of sketches detailing his experiences there. The principal theme is the development of a writer amid scenes of chaos and disruption. An offer was made to publish an anthology of the sketches in Paris in 1924, but the project never came to fruition.

A Young Doctor's Notebook

A Young Doctor's Notebook was drafted in 1919, then published mainly in medical journals between 1925–27. It is different in nature from Bulgakov's most famous works, being a first-person account of his experiences of treating peasants in his country practice, surrounded by ignorance and poverty, in a style reminiscent of another doctor and writer, Chekhov. Bulgakov learns by experience that often in this milieu what he has learnt in medical books and at medical school can seem useless, as he delivers babies, treats syphilitics and carries out amputations. The work is often published with *Morphine*, which describes the experience of a doctor addicted to morphine. This is autobiographical: it recalls Bulgakov's own period in medical service in Vyazma, in 1918, where, to alleviate his distress at the suffering he was seeing, he dosed himself heavily on his own drugs and temporarily became addicted to morphine.

Select Bibliography

Biographies:

Drawicz, Andrzey, *The Master and the Devil*, tr. Kevin Windle (New York, NY: Edwin Mellen Press, 2001)

Haber, Edythe C., *Mikhail Bulgakov: The Early Years* (Cambridge, MS: Harvard University Press, 1998)

Milne, Lesley, *Mikhail Bulgakov: A Critical Biography* (Cambridge: Cambridge University Press, 1990)

Proffer, Ellendea, *Bulgakov: Life and Work* (Ann Arbor, MI: Ardis, 1984)

Proffer, Ellendea, *A Pictorial Biography of Mikhail Bulgakov* (Ann Arbor, MI: Ardis, 1984)

Wright, A. Colin, *Mikhail Bulgakov: Life and Interpretation* (Toronto, ON: University of Toronto Press, 1978)

Letters, Memoirs:

Belozerskaya-Bulgakova, Lyubov, *My Life with Mikhail Bulgakov*, tr. Margareta Thompson (Ann Arbor, MI: Ardis, 1983)

Curtis, J.A.E., *Manuscripts Don't Burn: Mikhail Bulgakov: A Life in Letters and Diaries* (London: Bloomsbury, 1991)

Vozdvizhensky, Vyacheslav, ed., *Mikhail Bulgakov and his Times – Memoirs, Letters*, tr. Liv Tudge (Moscow: Progress Publishers, 1990)

ALMA CLASSICS

ALMA CLASSICS aims to publish mainstream and lesser-known European classics in an innovative and striking way, while employing the highest editorial and production standards. By way of a unique approach the range offers much more, both visually and textually, than readers have come to expect from contemporary classics publishing.

LATEST TITLES PUBLISHED BY ALMA CLASSICS

www.almaclassics.com

Gustave Flaubert	*Madame Bovary*
Ford Madox Ford	*The Good Soldier*
J.W. von Goethe	*The Sorrows of Young Werther*
Nikolai Gogol	*Petersburg Tales*
Thomas Hardy	*Tess of the d'Urbervilles*
Nathaniel Hawthorne	*The Scarlet Letter*
Henry James	*The Portrait of a Lady*
Franz Kafka	*The Metamorphosis and Other Stories*
D.H. Lawrence	*Lady Chatterley's Lover*
Mikhail Lermontov	*A Hero of Our Time*
Niccolò Machiavelli	*The Prince*
Edgar Allan Poe	*Tales of Horror*
Alexander Pushkin	*Eugene Onegin*
William Shakespeare	*Sonnets*
Mary Shelley	*Frankenstein*
Robert L. Stevenson	*Strange Case of Dr Jekyll and Mr Hyde and Other Stories*
Jonathan Swift	*Gulliver's Travels*
Antal Szerb	*Journey by Moonlight*
Leo Tolstoy	*Anna Karenina*
Ivan Turgenev	*Fathers and Children*
Mark Twain	*Adventures of Huckleberry Finn*
	The Adventures of Tom Sawyer
Oscar Wilde	*The Picture of Dorian Gray*
Virginia Woolf	*Mrs Dalloway*
Stefan Zweig	*A Game of Chess and Other Stories*

Printed in the USA
CPSIA information can be obtained
at www.ICGtesting.com
LVHW090301040324
773462LV00005B/406

9 780765 397133